Agnes L Ellis

Lights and Shadows of Sewickley Life

Memories of sweet valley

Agnes L Ellis

Lights and Shadows of Sewickley Life
Memories of sweet valley

ISBN/EAN: 9783337251659

Printed in Europe, USA, Canada, Australia, Japan

Cover: Foto ©Andreas Hilbeck / pixelio.de

More available books at **www.hansebooks.com**

SEWICKLEY, FROM ANDERSON'S HILL.

LIGHTS AND SHADOWS

OF

SEWICKLEY LIFE;

OR,

MEMORIES OF SWEET VALLEY.

BY

AGNES L. ELLIS.

" The friends thou hast, and their adoption tried,
Grapple them to thy soul with hooks of steel."
SHAKESPEARE.

PHILADELPHIA:
PRINTED BY J. B. LIPPINCOTT COMPANY.
1893.

Dedicated

TO

THE "BOYS AND GIRLS"

WHO SHARED THE SPORTS AND PLEASURES OF CHILDHOOD AND THE

CLOUDS AND SUNSHINE OF RIPER YEARS;

AND TO

THEIR SONS AND DAUGHTERS,

EACH ONE OF WHOM HAS A WARM CORNER IN THE

HEART OF

THE AUTHOR.

" Men are only boys grown tall,
Hearts don't change much after all."

LIST OF ILLUSTRATIONS.

PAGE

SEWICKLEY, FROM ANDERSON'S
HILL . . . . *Frontispiece*
JAMES McLAUGHLIN 25
RESIDENCE OF H. P. HERS-
PERGER 29
REV. JOSEPH S. TRAVELLI . . 43
JOHN R. GARRISON 59
BRUCE TRACY 59
J. P. KRAMER 63
ROBERT GLANCY 63
PHILO GOFF 63
WILLIAM RENO 63
REV. JOHN WHITE 67
REV. CHARLES THORN 71
REV. ROBERT HOPKINS . . . 75
M. E. CHURCHES 79
M. E. CHURCH 83
HON. J. W. F. WHITE . . . 87
JOHN N. WHITE, ESQ. . . . 87
JOHN JOHNSTON 91
B. C. CHRISTY, ESQ. 91
REV. H. L. CHAPMAN, D.D. . . 95
JOHN A. ROSENSTEEL 99
BUILT 1818 103
REV. D. E. NEVIN 107
REV. JAMES ALLISON 111
PRESBYTERIAN CHURCH . . . 115
REV. J. B. BITTINGER, D.D. . 119
REV. W. O. CAMPBELL, D.D. . 123
FIRST PRESBYTERIAN CHURCH 127

PAGE

WILLIAM WOODS, M.D. 131
GEORGE H. STARR 131
THEODORE H. NEVIN 135
ROBERT H. DAVIS 135
W. W. WATERS 139
LEETSDALE PRESBYTERIAN
CHURCH 143
REV. R. S. VAN CLEVE . . . 147
REV. JAMES L. REED 151
WILLIAM ABERCROMBIE . . . 155
SHIELDS' SCHOOL-HOUSE . . . 159
INTERIOR OF ST. STEPHEN'S
EPISCOPAL CHURCH 163
REV. ROBERT BENTON 167
ST. JAMES'S ROMAN CATHOLIC
CHURCH 171
REV. W. A. McKENZIE . . . 175
PROF. THOMAS E. WAKEHAM 175
ROBERT DICKSON 175
JOHN THOMPSON 175
ALEXANDER McELWAIN . . . 177
JAMES ELLIS 177
FRANK McCLELLAND 177
WILLIAM MILLER 177
REV. W. L. WALLACE, D.D. . 181
REV. A. G. WALLACE, D.D. . 183
FIRST UNITED PRESBYTERIAN
CHURCH 187
ELMER E. MILLER 189
FIRST BAPTIST CHURCH . . . 193

7

	PAGE		PAGE
Rev. John W. Moody	197	Robert P. Nevin	245
Jacob Boobyer, Jr.	199	Colonel John I. Nevin	263
John Dickson, M.D	205	Sewickley Station	271
John Way, Sr.	211	Samuel McCleery	275
D. L. S. Neely	215	Joseph W. Warren	279
Milton B. Goff	221	Hon. George H. Anderson	283
Hon. James M. Loughridge	225	John Patton, Jr.	287
C. S. Rinehart	229	Athletic Grounds	291
G. F. Muller	229	R. J. Murray, M.D.	301
William S. Dickson	233	John D. McCord, Jr.	301
Homer Jay Rose, A.M.	237	John B. Van Cleve	305
Hon. D. N. White	241		

PREFACE.

THE kind reception given to "Lights and Shadows of Sewickley Life," by both old and new residents, as well as many who had only had a passing glimpse of our beautiful Valley, has led me to yield to the request for another edition, "enlarged so as to embrace all the church history and other important matters not already noted."

It is very gratifying to hear from many sources that the historical facts and dates are all correct.

Although the research necessary has been an arduous task, the labor has been lightened and made pleasant by the renewal of friendships formed in childhood, as well as the many beautiful tributes (often from unlooked-for sources) to the memory of the parents to whose early training and devoted Christian lives I owe so much.

To all who have aided me in any way in regard to the "memories of the olden time," I hereby return sincere thanks.

It has been impossible to secure the portraits of some of the early residents, much to my regret.

To the old classmates into whose hands this may fall I extend a kindly greeting.

AGNES L. ELLIS.

SEWICKLEY. PA.

TESTIMONIALS.

We cull some of the kind words of friends from the many testimonials received:

"Miss A. L. Ellis:

"I am glad you are preparing a second and improved edition of your very interesting little book, 'Lights and Shadows of Sewickley Life.'

"It required much patience and industry to gather the facts and anecdotes of the early inhabitants, and you have woven them into a beautiful coronal, which should be highly prized by all their descendants, and be a bright ornament on the centre-table of every family in our Valley.

"It is well to preserve the faces and names and memories of our fathers and the incidents of local history. They are always interesting, and grow more interesting with passing years. They will be read and cherished long after you and I have passed away.

"J. W. F. White."

"Miss Agnes:

"I have read your book with much interest,—more, perhaps, than most of our Sewickley people,—for I am at a point of life where I have long stretches backward, and can see much more of the past than the young people of our now beautiful town.

"You have done a kindly thing in preserving in print the pleasant things of the 'long ago.' Surely, you deserve not credit only, but thanks also; and of both these I beg to express heartily my share.

"John Way, Jr.

"Sewickley, Pa."

11

"My Dear Miss Ellis:

"I have great pleasure in congratulating you on the conclusion of your historical sketches. As I believe that work done not simply as a task, but cheerfully, as a labor of love, and with painstaking effort to make it complete, even apart from the magnitude of the undertaking, deserves a generous reward, so I trust you may have yours from the community you have served. I feel confident that your history will be more fully appreciated with the lapse of years, when all who have been associated with the early history of the valley shall have passed away.

"Very truly yours,

"Wm. O. Campbell,

"Pastor First Presbyterian Church.

"Sewickley, Pa."

"My Dear Miss Ellis:

"It gives me great pleasure to know that you are about to publish some historical sketches of Sewickley and its surroundings. Local history should be preserved with great care.

"Memories fade, but records are permanent.

"The personal interest you have in our beautiful Valley will give vividness to your sketches.

"I cordially commend the work you have undertaken, and wish you success in your effort to keep fresh the memories of the past.   I am yours most truly,

"A. G. Wallace.

"Sewickley, Pa."

"My Dear Miss Ellis:

"May success attend your efforts: you deserve it!

"I am sure the new edition will be creditable alike to author and publisher, and will be welcomed by every loyal son and daughter of Sewickley.

"The 'lights and shadows' of half a century, which you have so faithfully and lovingly endeavored to fix upon the pages of your book, may not, probably will not, be a source of wealth, but they certainly will be a source of great pleasure to yourself and every true Sewickleyan.

"My own life in the beautiful Valley has been scarcely twenty years, yet do I feel that all its memories are a part of mine inheritance, so deeply and strongly have my associations taken root.

"I have, therefore, only words of commendation and encouragement for one who, in love and sympathy, is trying to preserve something of the landmarks, the every-day life, the flotsam past and present of Sewickley.   Yours very truly,
                                        "W. W. WATERS.
   "SEWICKLEY, PA."

"MY DEAR MISS ELLIS:

"I am glad that you are thinking of reprinting those 'old memories' of Sewickley. Such things become more valuable as years go by and the ranks of those who can remember the old times are thinned by death. In a place of such rapidly-changing population as Sewickley, it is doubly important and interesting that the 'old residents,' of whom we have so few, should preserve their recollections in some such permanent form as you have given to your reminiscences.
                        "Yours cordially,
                                "LUCY F. BITTINGER.
   "SEWICKLEY, PA."

"As an epitome of the village and the Valley, it is a work that must grow and deepen in interest as time passes, and thanks are due Miss Ellis for her labor, which was evidently one of love."— *East End Bulletin.*

"MY DEAR MISS ELLIS:

"I have been greatly pleased with and interested in your charming little book. It is a chapter of local history that will grow more valuable with every year.
                        "MRS. E. A. WADE (Bessie Bramble).
   "EDGEWOODVILLE."

"We are reading your delightful little book like Miss Mitford's 'Our Village.'   Cordially yours,
                                "PERRY MASON & CO.
   "BOSTON, MASS."

"Dear Miss Ellis:

"I am greatly obliged for the copy of 'Lights and Shadows of Sewickley Life' sent to Washington. I have been looking over it this morning with a great deal of interest.

"Yours truly. M. S. Quay."

"To those who have been long familiar with the Valley, your beautiful book, 'Lights and Shadows of Sewickley Life,' must prove quite a treasure. J. S. Bracken, D.D.,

"Pastor Union M. E. Church, Allegheny, Pa."

"The thoughts are well matured, beautifully clothed, and so natural that one feels as though they were by your side, living the days of youth over again.

"Mrs. J. S. Bracken."

"My Dear Friend:

"I enjoyed reading the 'Sweet Valley' very much, and it recalled many pleasant as well as the sad memories of the past.

"I sent several copies to old friends, and also to some of the pupils of 'Sewickley Academy.' All who saw and read the little book were much interested in it, and grateful to the author for recalling the happy school-days with so many pleasant associations. Your friend,

"Eliza I. T. Glenn.

"Wooster, Ohio."

"I wish you great success with your venture. You have a wide and interesting field for your book.

"Very sincerely yours,

"W. H. Locke.

"East Liverpool, Ohio."

"Dear Friend:

"Would that the spirit had moved you to begin your work several years sooner.

"The venerable white heads are disappearing one by one, and with them the recollections of those earlier years of hardship and noble endeavor.

"To gather these memories must be an interesting work, and the gift of preserving them for future generations is an enviable one. That you may be entirely successful, is the sincere wish of

"MRS. P. D. NICOLS.

"SEWICKLEY. PA."

CHAPTER I.

" Happy the man, from busy cares withdrawn,
Who seeks the sweets of rural ease,
Where every spot hath power to please."

EWICKLEY, a borough of nearly 5000 inhabitants, on the bank of the Ohio River, twelve miles below Pittsburg, is a very different place from the Sewickley we knew before the days of railroads, telegraph, and telephones.

The first time that Sewickley appears in history is in connection with Colonel Morgan, a native of Philadelphia, Pa., who commanded the first military company sent by that city to take part in the war of the Revolution. He was sent to Fort Pitt as an Indian agent.

The Delaware Indians, who then occupied the Valley, in gratitude for kindness received at his hands, offered as a free gift, to him and his children, "all the ground from the hills to the river, for a distance of six miles." Although deeply touched by their kindness, Colonel Morgan declined to accept this reward for "merely doing his duty."

By a treaty made October 23, 1784, at Fort Stanwix, the six nations—viz., the Mohawks, Oneidas, Onondagas, Senecas, Cayugas, and Tuscaroras—sold to Penn the lands north and west of the Ohio and Allegheny Rivers.

This treaty was ratified by the Wyandots and Dela-
wares in January, 1785.

By Act of March 12, 1783, anticipating above purchase, part of said lands, including those on which
Sewickley now stands, was set aside

"For the redemption of the Certificates of Depreciation given to the officers and soldiers of the Pennsylvania
Line, in pursuance of an Act of December 18, 1780,
providing that the certificates should be equal to gold or
silver in payment of unlocated lands, if the owners
should think proper to purchase such."

The Act of 1780 was passed to encourage enlistment
and reward those who in the Revolutionary War entered
the military service in the Pennsylvania Line and the
State Navy.

An order for the survey of these lands was issued to
the Surveyor-General, June 10, 1783. The lands were
divided into districts for convenience of survey, and
Sewickley was in the Second Depreciation District, which
was assigned to Daniel Leet. Through the knowledge
of the country thus obtained, Daniel Leet secured possession of that large and valuable body of lands on the
Sewickley bottom which descended to his daughter, the
late Mrs. Shields, wife of David Shields.

The first lands sold in Leet's district went at the
average price of eight shillings five pence, or about two
dollars per acre. These sales were made at the "Old
Coffee-House," Philadelphia.

In 1786, Mr. Daniel Leet owned the tracts numbered
7, 8, and 9. In 1791 he owned, in addition to these,
numbers 3, 4, 5, and 6.

The names given in the original patents to these tracts owned by Mr. Daniel Leet were: 3, Newbury; 4, Norwich; 5, Newington; 6, Lincoln; 7, Locust Bottom; 8, Sugar Bottom; 9, Leetsburg.

No. 2, a tract of two hundred acres, adjoining the present borough limits and extending to what is now called Edgeworth Avenue, was purchased from the State, in 1785, by Mr. Caleb Way, of Chester County, at the sale in Philadelphia, and was occupied by his son John Way (grandfather of John Way, Jr.) in 1797.

Mr. Way occupied a log-house, which stood near the site of the Sewickley gas-works at Quaker Valley, until his new house was completed.

It was built in 1810, and, being the only brick house between Pittsburg and Beaver, was spoken of as "*the brick house.*" It is now occupied by Mr. Hay Walker.

In talking over old times with one of Sewickley's oldest residents lately, he told me that during the memorable time when the spotted fever, or "black plague," raged in this vicinity, Squire Way and his wife, who lived in "the brick house," were the only persons willing to venture near the smitten ones; so, when every one else refused to enter the dwellings of the fever patients, they kept two horses saddled night and day, riding here and there, ministering to the sick and dying and caring for the dead. Such heroism is worthy of record, that those who never knew them in the flesh may be influenced by the spirit which led them.

The first white settler in Sewickley borough was Henry Ulery, a German sea-captain, who loved to recall his adventures and perilous sea-voyages for the entertainment of those who came to be his neighbors in after years.

The tract of land No. 1, called Loretta, was purchased at the government sale at Philadelphia by Levi Hollingsworth, who, before receiving the patent for it, transferred it to Mark Wilcox, January 19, 1786, who, December 6, 1786, conveyed it to Jonathan Leet. On the 10th of April, 1798, Jonathan Leet sold it to Henry Ulery.

Heretofore the Indians had had full possession, and for many years after the land was sold, the "trail" was seen across the river, and after they had left the canoes on this side, running past the property now owned by Mrs. R. H. Davis. The narrow path was called for years, "Wheelbarrow Alley."

Henry Ulery built a log-house on the bank of the river, not far from the spot now occupied by Park Place Hotel.

He had some pretty sharp battles with the Indians, who he felt were invading his rights, as they were in the habit of helping themselves to corn and other articles of which they were in need.

But what of the Indian's rights? As they were driven from place to place, no doubt their thoughts were like those of the Indian hunter,—

"Oh, why does the white man follow my path
　　Like a hound on the tiger's track?
Does the flush on my dark skin waken his wrath?
　　Does he covet the bow at my back?
There are rivers and seas where billows and breeze
　　Bear riches for him alone,
And the sons of the wood never plunge in the flood
　　Which the white man calls *his own.*"

Mrs. Ulery was very tender and kind to the red men, and often supplied their wants during the absence of her husband.

Wishing for better water than the river supplied, Mr. Ulery commenced to dig a well. After the workmen had gone down a number of feet, a rain-storm came on and put a stop to the work. Two of the children, taking advantage of the rope that was left hanging from the windlass, arranged it for a swing. The younger of the two wandered off, leaving the other, a very little fellow, swinging contentedly. After a time the elder one was missed, and searched for in vain. At last, in the half-dug well, which contained a good quantity of water from the recent rain, the little one was found—dead.

The stone for building up the well was brought from the other side of the river (a little distance below) in a canoe.

During one of these trips, when a boy who worked for Mr. Henry Ulery was crossing with his load, a sudden storm came up, and the canoe was upset, the boy being drowned.

These two calamities had a very depressing effect upon the mind of Mrs. Ulery, and, as they were not very prosperous during the years they were on that farm, she, saying their bad fortune was all because of the dreadful well, persuaded her husband to sell out.

A short time ago, Mrs. Ringley, daughter of Mr. Tracy, who bought three acres of that old tract, including the spot occupied by the cabin and well, gave me a drink from that old well, which is now ninety-five years old, with its walls still in good condition. It is regularly cleaned, kept in repair, and used by Mr. Ringley's family.

Henry Ulery sold the farm in 1810 to Thomas Hoey, grandfather of Mrs. Judge White and Mrs. Harbaugh, of this place. In the Recorder's office in Pittsburg we find in an old volume,—" Henry Ulery sold to Thomas Hoey, for the sum of $4000, lawful money of the U. S., ... a piece of land situate in Ohio Township, Allegheny County, and Commonwealth aforesaid, called ' Leretto,' in Leet's district, No. 1, beginning at a hoop ash tree on the bank of the Ohio River, thence by lot No. 2, the property of John Way, Esq., north forty-nine and a half degrees, east two hundred and seventy-five perches, to a white oak saplin on the bank of said river, thence down the same, four hundred and twenty perches, to the place of beginning.''

Mr. Hoey lived in the log house until the stone house, near the same spot, which he occupied for years, was built. His home was a stopping-place for all the ministers who sought refuge for themselves and food and shelter for their horses.

Among the childish memories which his daughter, Mrs. Thorn, loved to recall to her children, were those in connection with the large sugar camp below the hotel. It was all such a time of delight, from the time the sweet water was collected until the time when the delicious syrup was taken from the kettles.

Mr. Hoey's farm and the adjoining land, owned by Mr. Beer, extended from Osburn to Quaker Valley, where the farm of Squire Way (grandfather of Mr. John Way) began.

Father McClelland, the first Methodist preacher in the Valley, often put up there.

At the foot of the stairway, standing by the window in a room fronting on the river, in that stone house, Rev. Charles Thorn and Miss Sophronia, daughter of Thomas Hoey, were married.

Mr. Thomas Beer bought a large tract of land adjoining that of Mr. Hoey's in 1802 from "John Vail and Sarah his wife."

The division line of these two tracts was in early times called "Graveyard Lane," from the fact that the acre of ground on the south into which this lane, running directly north and south and separating the two farms of Mr. Hoey and Mr. Beer, entered, had been given by these two gentlemen during the plague of 1809–10 that the inhabitants might have a place to bury their dead.

The tract owned by Mr. Beer had been purchased from the government by Henry Pratt in 1786, who, September 7, 1793, sold it to Jonathan Leet. April 7, 1802, Jonathan Leet sold it to John Vail, who, in 1810, sold it to Thomas Beer. That tract of land was called Aleppo, and contained two hundred and thirty-four acres, ninety-one perches.

The tract adjoining, consisting of two hundred and five acres, also belonged to Mr. Pratt. It was owned for many years by James Park and his son. Osburn Borough occupies much of the Park farm; it contains many handsome residences, owned by Messrs. Thomas Hare, James Arrott, Marshall McDonald, and others.

William McLaughlin, great-grandfather of Mrs. P. D. Nicols, of our borough, bought a tract of land from the government, in 1798, several miles back of the borough limits, in what is now called Sewickley Township.

He is described as being a tall, stately gentleman, of commanding appearance. He married a Miss McMichael. In 1820 he taught a private school near the home of Mr. Jacob Fry, who after his death succeeded him as teacher. Mr. McLaughlin was a well-educated man for the time in which he lived, and had much force of character.

Mr. James McLaughlin, his son, whose portrait we give, is remembered by many of the old residents of the borough. He was connected with its first religious organizations, a godly man, and "wonderfully gifted in prayer." He and his wife, who was a daughter of Colonel Campbell, lived on the old farm with their three children for many years.

Mr. McLaughlin was highly respected by all in the neighborhood, and to many of those who brought their grievances, fancied or real, to him, he acted the part of " peacemaker," sending those who had come as enemies away in the most friendly relations.

Mr. William McLaughlin was a Scotch-Irishman, who came from the East, travelling over the mountains in one of the so-called " bell-teams," an immense covered wagon drawn by six horses, all decorated with bells.

The original name was McGlachlin. They had four children,—James, whom we have already mentioned ; William, the father of Louise McLaughlin, the famous artist and author; John, who enlisted and was never heard from after the battle of "Orleans;" and Ann, who became Mrs. Gordon, mother of Rev. James Gordon, late of Eldorado, Kansas.

JAMES McLAUGHLIN.

In 1805 Robert Linn came from Ireland, and soon after settled on the farm near Mr. McLaughlin, which is now owned by his son Hugh, who is living in a substantial frame house not many rods from the spot where the old house stood in which he was born eighty years ago. Mrs. Hugh Linn, who was Miss Ann S. Dé Putron, came with her father's family from Guernsey Island to America in 1830. After stopping at Cleveland, they travelled from there to Pittsburg in a "bell-team," stopping over night at Fife's Hotel, the building on Beaver Street afterwards used by Mr. Travelli for an academy.

Some years after, Mr. Dé Putron returned with his family to Sewickley and bought from Mr. John Fife (grandfather of Dr. Thomas Grimes, of this place) the cottage which he had built in 1834 and thirty acres of ground, where deer and wild ducks sported in great abundance.

Mr. Thomas Hoey died in that house one Sunday morning in the summer of 1838, where he had been carefully and tenderly nursed by his daughter, Mrs. Fife, during his last illness. This house, now owned and occupied by Mr. W. P. Hersperger, is the oldest house in the borough.

Mrs. Elizabeth Grimes was married in the cottage in 1834, soon after its completion. Her father, John Fife, Jr., was the son of John Fife, of Upper St. Clair Township, Allegheny County, one of the two pioneer brothers who came to that region in 1793 from Scotland.

John Fife, Jr., the owner of the cottage and hotel, had lived near New Lisbon, Ohio, where Mrs. Grimes was born, removing to Sewickley in 1824.

Mrs. Linn, who was married in the cottage in 1839, by Rev. John White, says that, although an addition was built to the back of the house, the front, the main building, is very little changed. It was a frame house, painted cream color, with green trimmings.

When being shown through the house lately by Mrs. Hersperger, we came to the low-ceiled room over the parlor, the play-room of her little six-year-old daughter, by whose tiny hands it is kept in beautiful order, a story told by those connected with the cottage in early times came to mind.

After Mr. Dé Putron's family had taken possession of their new home, Mr. John Fife, the former owner, paid them a visit, and said, "I sold you the house and all its belongings, with one exception; come with me." Going to the upper room, which was lined with narrow boards, "ploughed and grooved," with no sign of an opening anywhere, he walked to one corner and, lifting out a short board, reached in his hands and drew out a bag of gold and silver so heavy that it taxed his strength to carry it.

When Mr. Dé Putron moved to his house on the hill, near the present residence of Mrs. John Fleming, Dr. William Woods came from Pittsburg and took possession. There, Mr. Charles G. Woods, of Osborn Borough, well known to all our citizens, was born.

The first store-keepers in Sewickley were Robert and James Green, who came from the East and opened a general country store in a log-house which stood fronting the Beaver Road, just where Grimes Street commences, by the Baptist Church.

RESIDENCE OF M. P. HERSPERGER.

BUILT BY JOHN FITE, 1814

In a short time James returned to his home east of the mountains, and Robert built a frame house on a lot which he had bought from Mr. John Little. Two of Mr. Green's daughters now occupy the house, which adjoins the residence of Mr. Franks, on Beaver Street.

Robert married Miss Eliza Smith, grand-daughter of Mr. Bean, of the Valley, now called Leetsdale.

The oldest resident of the borough is Mr. Jacob F. Ringley, now in his ninety-third year. He came to Sewickley in 1848. He is a native of Germany.

The oldest resident *born* in the Valley is Mr. John Larimore, now eighty years old. He was born at Leetsdale, and remembers much about the early days, when all that was cleared of the Valley was almost one immense corn-field, the ground producing "*sick wheat*," and the oats growing so rank that they fell and rotted. Between the rows of corn, the Spanish needles and Jersey weed flourished so abundantly that, before the corn could be pulled up (which was the mode instead of cutting) and thrown out on the heap ready for husking, a boy had to be mounted on a horse dragging *brush* between the rows to clear out the intruders.

Mr. William Larimore, father of John Larimore, moved to Sewickley Bottom, now Leetsdale, just one hundred years ago.

Mr. Nathan McPherson, grandfather of Mr. Robert L. McPherson, who was one of our "brave soldier-boys," was another of the very early settlers at or before the time of Mr. Larimore.

Rev. Thomas McClelland bought the farm on which his son Louis now lives in his seventy-ninth year, in

1810. It is situated six miles to the north-east of the borough. The ground cost one dollar and twenty-five cents an acre.

Mr. McClelland was the first Methodist to hold religious services in Pittsburg, preaching in a foundry near "the Point," I am informed by his son. He organized the first class in Sewickley Valley, in the house of Jesse Fisher, which was also a regular preaching place for the Methodists until the frame meeting-house, which was used for a number of years, was built near Mr. Leet's mill.

Another old resident who lived near Mr. McClelland was Mr. Basil Davis, who had purchased his farm for twenty-five cents an acre. He carried on sugar-making, as there were quite a number of sugar-maple trees on his farm, for each pound of which he received twenty-five cents; so each pound of sugar just paid for an acre of land. Not far from that farm was another which, as an old resident puts it, "was bought for three hams of meat." Still another, a tract of three hundred acres, was paid for with a horse. This tract, exactly north-east of Sewickley Borough, comprises two of the best farms in the neighborhood to-day.

Mr. Thomas Neill came to Sewickley in 1830. He was a native of Ballymena, Ireland.

Mrs. Jacob Whitesell, mother of Frank Whitesell, Esq., was a daughter of Mr. Neill. The farm on which she spent her girlhood was a few miles back of the village.

Mr. John Little bought the farm owned by Mr. John Hoey, one of Thomas Hoey's children, in 1832. The house occupied by Mr. Hoey stood about on the site of

Dr. Jennings's house, corner of Beaver and Walnut Streets.

Mr. Samuel Little, his son, resides near the site of the house in which his father kept a travellers' hotel for many years.

Many of the farms, among which may be mentioned those of Frederick Merriman, Jacob Fry, Captain Murray, and the one on which Mr. Besterman has lived for the past twenty-five years, were originally comprised in the twelve hundred acres which James Moore, grandfather of Mr. John Moore, usually called "Commodore Moore," owned at one time on these Sewickley hills.

James Moore belonged to the Buffalo Valley, and was one of General Washington's scouts during the Revolutionary War. Besides these twelve hundred acres, we find it on record that he owned six thousand acres in Kentucky.

It shows something of the character of the man, as we remember the story about the Indian whose tomahawk grazed his side as he hurled it from his covert at the white man, when, upon searching for and finding the Indian, himself wounded and helpless, Mr. Moore conveyed him to a place of safety, and, like the good Samaritan, bound up his wounds and nursed him back to health.

John, one of Mr. Moore's sons, who died out on the old farm twelve hours after he was bitten by a rattlesnake, was on his way to the new possessions, his sister Mary accompanying his family. When somewhere on the mountains, as they travelled slowly along, Jacob Fry, a lover of Mary's, riding on horseback, overtook the party,

and offered her on the spot his heart and hand, begging
for an early marriage.

Now, it was never known that any command of the
stately father, who, arrayed in his cloak and hat, with his
military bearing and commanding appearance, inspired
his children with awe, was ever disobeyed; so Mary replied, "I will never marry you until you bring me the
written consent of my parents."

Quickly the horse's head was turned towards the home
of the brave scout, and before the party reached their
journey's end, Jacob presented himself with the necessary document, and erelong received his reward.

To Frederick Merriman, James Moore gave "three
hundred acres, more or less," of his large farm, for a
gun, an iron kettle, and a sled. This farm was situated
on the hill at the head of "Turkey-foot Run." His son
lives in the same house in which his father lived in 1810.
To another he gave one hundred acres for three hams.

About 1813, a nervous, timid man saw one of the
settlers, wearing a coonskin cap and carrying a cane,
going into a neighbor's house on the farm (Mr. Merriman's), and as there were still two or three Indians
roaming about, and not seeing the face of the white man,
he ran, telling that an Indian had gone in and killed all
the family. All the settlers in the neighborhood fled
for their lives, some of them escaping over the river, and
fearing to return until informed by the unsuspecting
family, after a time, of the true state of affairs.

When Mr. Thomas Hamilton's family came from
Pittsburg to take possession of their farm, they put up
at Mr. Linn's, a brother-in-law's house. Mr. William

Hamilton, one of the sons (father of Captain Thomas Hamilton), was then a child of seven years of age.

The morning after their arrival, he was frightened upon seeing all the men in the surrounding country armed with axes, hatchets, etc., collecting. They set to work felling trees and hewing logs, and by night-fall the house of one room was finished, and the family took possession of it. In that house Mr. Robert Glancy was born, and it stood until lately on the farm now owned by the children of the late Dr. Douglass.

The gun which was given in part payment to Mr. Moore for the three hundred acres had been a companion of Frederick Merriman both in peace and war. He was one of General Wayne's soldiers, and afterwards became a squatter on the farm which Mr. William McLaughlin had purchased from the State, being the first white settler on the Sewickley Hills. He was offered for the gun forty acres of land in " Allegheny Town," comprising the spot now occupied by City Hall, Carnegie Library, etc., but refused the offer, and made a bargain with Mr. Moore for the farm.

Mr. Mitchell and Mr. Means both purchased farms in the same neighborhood in 1813. Mrs. Rebecca Dickson lives on the old Mitchell farm, and Mr. Joseph Means, brother of Miss Susan Means of our borough, lives on the farm owned by his father.

In 1846, thirty houses, dotted here and there for a distance of more than a mile, with two small churches (a Methodist and a Presbyterian), made up the town.

I promised to give you some memories of the early days of our now thriving town. Some of them are per-

sonal memories. Many of them came to me through
the words of long ago, uttered by the lips of those now
done with our commonplace language, but the influence
of whose beautiful lives yet lingers, with some of those
who still inhabit this, to them, fairest and dearest spot
on earth. Said one who came many years ago to find a
home here, "Sweet Valley! never fairer scene burst upon
the vision of the traveller than that upon which our eyes
rested as, after a long journey, which our quiet horses
had made leisurely, we rested in view of the lovely spot
which was to be our future home."

The small village was composed of many nationali-
ties, from the lowliest toilers to the man of wealth; an
industrious, happy people.

I remember seeing a letter, that had travelled some
hundreds of miles, directed to "Sweet Valley or Switley-
ville." It came all right with its queer directions, and
"Sweet Valley" has always seemed since then to tell
the story of the place, which, "beautiful for situation,"
has a charm for the long absent resident, causing him to
revisit again and again the scenes of his youth.

The only means of reaching the adjacent cities and
towns prior to 1851 (the year the railroad was finished), except when we were fortunate enough to catch
a throughgoing stage, was by an occasional steamboat
going up and down the Ohio River. A large house near
the boat-landing was our waiting place for the oft-times
long delayed boat (where the wave of a handkerchief
was the signal that the boat was expected to land), and
often there were hours of waiting, when the hostess
insisted upon giving food as well as shelter.

The first boat built for the Western waters is said to have been the "New Orleans," built at Pittsburg in 1811.

For many years keel-boats were used, and some of the old inhabitants remember hearing the cheery songs of the keel-boatmen as they labored at their tasks going up and down the Ohio. The number of keel-boats employed on the upper Ohio is said to have been one hundred and fifty. It required a month to make the trip between Pittsburg and Louisville.

Steamboats were used in 1817. The first one that came to this place from Cincinnati was the "Constitution," but it never reached Pittsburg, as it ran aground on the bar at "Dead Man." Two years afterwards the machinery was hauled away.

The first boat with a whistle passed Sewickley in 1837. It was called the "Uncle Sam," and there are still some of the early residents left who remember the excitement in Sewickley and vicinity when its shrill tones were first heard.

Mr. Cadwallader Evans, father of the late George Evans, who lived in Mr. Dickson's house on Hill Street, had worked for years, and at last received a patent for the steam-whistle. It was arranged above the boiler, so that the engineer could control it.

The boat ran aground in "White's Riffle," near the old Tracy Landing, and the whistle was blown again and again. Through the valley and over the hill-top it echoed and re-echoed, causing a feeling of terror and alarm. Mr. Jacob Fry announced to his family and neighbors that the end of the world had come, and Gabriel was blowing his trumpet, telling them to fall on their knees and improve the short time left in prayer. A general belief was that it was the cry of a wildcat; so some of the men left their sugar-making and ran here and there with pitchforks, while Moses Hendricks, accompanied by a friend, took his gun and went as far as "Crow's Run" to shoot the animal. At last word was brought from the neighbors near the river what was the cause of the outcry, and quiet and peace were restored.

A writer in an old volume says, in speaking of our beautiful river, in 1843, "The Allegheny comes down with a strong current from the north-east and, sweeping suddenly round to the north-west, receives the more gentle current of the Monongahela from the south, their combined waters flowing on to the Mississippi under the name of the Ohio or Beautiful River.

"The aborigines and the French considered the Allegheny and Ohio to be the same stream, and the Monongahela to be a tributary. 'Allegheny' being a word in the Delaware language, and 'O-hee-o,' in the Seneca, both meaning fair water. Hence the French term 'Belle Rivière' was only a translation of the Indian name."

The first steamboat to tow coal from Pittsburg to New Orleans was the "Crescent City," in 1854. It was owned by George Leslie. Captain John Cochran was the commander, and Captain McCormick, now of Leetsdale, was the mate.

Mr. Cadwallader Evans's patent was for an escapevalve connected with the engine, so arranged that, as soon as there was too much steam "aboard," the whistle gave the alarm. The engineer, and not the pilot, as nowadays, had in those times the management of the whistle. What warm and lasting friendships were formed during those hours of waiting and travel.

One of the citizens tried for a time making daily trips from this place to Pittsburg with an omnibus, but it was not a successful enterprise.

The Indians called the water Seweekly that ran from the maple trees, meaning sweet water, and for a time the trees were called by the old residents "*Seweekly trees.*" Gradually the streams were called Seweekly, and we now know them as Big Sewickley and Little Sewickley Creeks.

The name "Sewickleyville" was decided on in the autumn of 1840. Previously, "Contention," "Fifetown," and "Bowling Green" were among the names by which it was called.

When it had been decided, at a meeting held for the purpose, to name the village *Sewickleyville* and drop all the other names, the men and boys prepared for a regular jubilee. Procuring some tar barrels, they ran long poles through openings in the ends, and, setting fire to the barrels, ran, holding the poles, up and down Beaver Street, then called Beaver Road, shouting "*Sewickleyville! Sewickleyville!*" and the name given with a fiery baptism is very sweet to our ears.

When Zachary Taylor, our chief magistrate, and his party travelled through this place in carriages in 1849, the citizens had a much better opportunity of seeing him than if he had made a flying trip through by rail. After driving leisurely through the village, bowing pleasantly to the people who had come out to see him pass,—being loudly and heartily cheered by the Academy boys,—he drove into the grounds at Edgeworth Seminary, where a song of greeting was responded to by a speech.

The next stop was at Economy, where a piece of silk-velvet brocade, sufficient for a dress for Mrs. Taylor (the result of an industry that has since been abandoned in the quaint old town), was presented by Miss Rapp.

The house in which I write to-day is built in what the boys and girls in those days called "the woods;" and, while now the centre, was at that time on the outskirts of the town. Two trees, within sight of my window, still stand as venerable patriarchs, rearing their stately heads and extending their arms as if in benediction.

What good times the boys and girls had then! All these so-called "woods" were common property. No one thought of interfering with them as they roamed here and there in search of nuts or berries.

During one of these berrying excursions to "Anderson's Hill," the boys and girls, having gathered a goodly supply of the tempting fruit, were resting on a grassy slope before starting for home. One of the little girls had thrown her hat on the ground at a little distance,—a hat of coarse braids of straw trimmed with a band of green ribbon. A cow, quietly feeding at a short distance, had gradually approached until she had reached the hat. A scream from little Mary, and the words "Oh, my hat!" caused us all to look quickly around, and there we saw the cow composedly chewing the straw hat, unmindful of our shouting and running. After the poor child had become reconciled to her loss and we were on our way home, what we thought of most was how old

Brindle, as she lay down to blink and meditate and chew the cud, was going to prepare the green ribbon for digestion.

One of the most enjoyable of these excursions was in the neighborhood of a wonderful Indian cave, on a hill back of the town, which some of the more venturesome explored from time to time. A sort of rude ladder was contrived, and descending this to the depth of perhaps ten or twelve feet a long, narrow passage led to a place something like a gateway, very narrow, called "the fat man's misery." It was quite an effort for some of us to get through it.

I remember we often saw the boys from the village Academy, on their half-holidays, with long ropes and candles in hand going to the cave, which they were supposed to explore to a greater depth than others, which fact made us think them very brave.

Our village was noted for two of the best schools within many miles of Pittsburg,—an Academy for boys and a Seminary for girls. Here were gathered representatives of many families, North, South, East, and West.

In 1838, Professor Wm. Nevin and John B. Champ began the Sewickley Academy in "*the brick house*," at Quaker Valley. Rev. Joseph S. Travelli took charge of it when it was removed to the village, he having returned from his missionary work on account of the ill-health of Mrs. Travelli. This was in 1842. The Academy building, with its spacious grounds, stood near the corner of Beaver and Fife Streets.

The Edgeworth Seminary was opened in 1836 by

Mrs. Mary Oliver, an English lady, who previously had a school at Braddocksfield.

Mrs. Oliver was dearly loved by her pupils and deeply mourned at her death. Her pupils erected to her memory the first monument that was seen in the Sewickley grave-yard, back of the Presbyterian Church. It was removed to the new cemetery, and there to-day we read these words, among others inscribed in loving memory,—"Her best epitaph is the title 'Mother' in the hearts of all her pupils."

The Seminary was conducted for many years after, first, under the care of Rev. D. E. Nevin, and afterwards Professor Williams, Dr. H. R. Wilson, and Rev. Aaron Williams. It was destroyed by fire some years ago, and not rebuilt.

Many of the leading business men of Pittsburg and vicinity were educated in the old Academy, and homes far and near are cheered and blest by the wives and mothers who, along with a knowledge of mathematics, English literature, music, painting, etc., learned many beautiful lessons of love and good-will in the quiet Seminary nestled among the maple trees.

The scholars from the respective schools walked decorously, two by two, marshalled by the sedate-looking teachers. If perchance they crossed each other's pathway, many a stolen glance and word were exchanged, and occasionally a little note found its way through the fingers of some urchin, all unconscious of wrong-doing, from one fond heart to another.

About midway between the old Academy in the village and the Seminary at Edgeworth stood a famous old

REV. JOSEPH S. TRAVELLI.

sycamore tree. The course of the Little Sewickley Creek has been changed, but then it emptied into the Ohio River, near the spot where the old tree stood, not far from the present Quaker Valley Station. It was seven feet in diameter, with a door on one side rounded at the top, and seven or eight feet from the ground a sort of roof of boards, which also served as a floor for the boys who were venturesome enough to use the *second story* room. The tree was dug and *burned* out until the benches which were arranged in the circular room below would accommodate quite a little party.

Mrs. Wm. Miller, Mrs. Hugh Linn, and Mrs. Jacob Ringley all remember their visits to the tree; Mrs. Linn saying a party of half a dozen persons often took possession of it.

It was used by the Academy boys and Seminary girls as a post-office, and many a precious missive found its way into the hiding-place to await its owner.

A poor family who were in great straits at one time took possession of this primitive home, much to the discomforture of the young people.

I remember, when a child, being impressed with a feeling of awe whenever the teacher of French in the Academy, an old, reverend-looking gentleman, met us in his solitary walks. Always, with a peculiar gesture, he said, if as usual we were laughing and talking, " Be wise !"

Strange to say, the names of the other teachers in the Academy were as familiar to us as " household words," and we knew no other name for him than " Mr. Be Wise."

What wonderful soirées the Seminary girls used to give, and like a beautiful echo from the past come to us the voices of some of those who sang. For a time they gladdened earth's homes, and then joined the throng of " winged choristers."

One of these, whose gift as a poet was known to but few during her school-days, has, during the past few years, as her heart responded in sympathy with the joys and sorrows of friends and neighbors, sung of them in touching strains.

Mrs. Jennie Davis Miller, whose *pen name* was "Virginia Dare," was an honor to Sewickley. Her beautiful Christian character was a rebuke to the selfish and worldly, her love and friendship were to us a comfort and joy. Her death, which occurred in April, 1892, caused an aching void in many hearts.

Remembering that her first morning in heaven was Easter morning, we read with especial interest the following poem :

EASTER.

" *He is risen, as He said.*"

Shine, Easter sun, just risen, shine on,
Till all the shades of night are gone,
As " Sun of Righteousness" doth shine,—
Our risen Lord,—the Christ Divine.

Glad streams from icy thrall set free,
Haste to the rivers and the sea ;
And as ye go the message speed :
" The Lord is risen—is risen indeed."

Oh! first fair flowers now blossoming,
Oh! happy birds that soar and sing,
Released from winter's grave and prison,
Assure sad souls, "The Lord is risen."

Ye little flowers, whose opening eyes
Are blue with blue of heav'nly skies,
Say, sweetest flowers, with perfumed breath,
"The Lord is risen—He conquers death."

The seed, though buried, does not die,
Nor in its grave forgotten lie.
Oh! sorrowing souls, lift up your eyes:
"The Lord is risen"—your dead shall rise.

VIRGINIA DARE.

The exhibition at the close of each half-yearly term at the Academy was an event to which the whole village looked forward with eager interest, because the whole village was invited, and generally availed themselves of the opportunity to attend; the Principal, dear, good man, having a word of welcome for all, rich and poor.

How plainly I seem to see some of those youthful orators now. One of them has for years been connected with railroads, and has well-nigh forgotten the time when an immense farm-wagon was loaded with trunks, *en route* for Pittsburg, the day after school closed, that being the only baggage-car known in our quiet village. While he now talks of stocks and dividends, I fancy I recall the youthful features, and hear yet the echo of the words in his impersonation of William Tell, as he drew forth the concealed arrow, "To shoot *thee*, tyrant, had I slain my *son*."

Fire destroyed the old Academy building, on Beaver

Street, in 1851, and the school was removed to the building now known as " Park Place Hotel ;" but, as we pass the old grounds, we seem to see the boys at play, and recall the youthful features of some of them.

About five o'clock in the morning the fire broke out, and yet at that early hour almost the whole population was on the spot in a few minutes.

Some very ridiculous things occurred in the anxiety of every one to save something. One old gentleman seized an axe, and with vigorous blows brought down a long pole on which some of the boys had placed a martin-box.

Henry Ward Beecher once said that the birds had family worship at four o'clock in the morning ; and in these days, since our English cousins, the sparrows, have populated the leafy part of the town, I often fancy they are at that early hour having a sort of *camp meeting ;* but, as I was going to say, the birds, parents and children (worship being over), had likely gone out for their morning constitutional, and thus escaped the sudden awakening our friend had in store for them.

Since the Seminary became a thing of the past only, and Mr. Travelli's Academy was closed, an Academy for boys and girls was conducted for a number of years, first in the old Presbyterian Church building, and afterwards in the beautiful building erected by Mr. John Way, Jr., on Beaver Street, just at the end of the borough line.

Under Mr. Way's own care, with a number of able teachers, this school was conducted for a number of years very successfully ; and it is hoped that some day it may reopen its doors to a band of young men and women seeking a higher education than the public school affords without the necessity of leaving home.

While the friend of every right movement for the good of the community, Mr. Way's grandest work has been among the young men of the place. Scores of them, receiving instruction in the Bible-class, supplemented by a lively interest in everything concerning their home-life and week-day employments, have been led to take a grander and more solemn view of life, its duties and responsibilities.

The village boasted very few stores as I first remember it, but I fancy I see each store-keeper, and the general arrangements of the stores. The principal one was a dry-goods and grocery store combined, a regular country store, kept by Mr. George H. Starr, an elder in the Presbyterian Church, and one of the most honest, upright, and godly of men. At that time an elder's duties and responsibilities were considered *hardly* second to those of the minister, and in the command to have an oversight of the flock, the words were taken literally. Faithfully and well did he perform his obligations.

Mr. Starr came from Michigan to Sewickley to be a teacher of mathematics in the Academy kept by Messrs. Nevin and Champ, but after a time gave up his profession and opened the store. He married Miss Rachel Hooker, a teacher in the Seminary, whose memory is associated with all that is good and true.

Mr. Starr was born near Ballston Spa, N. Y., and Mrs. Starr was born in Utica, N. Y. The influence of these two devoted Christian workers is far reaching as eternity. Truly "the memory of the just is blessed."

4

He was the village squire, too, but, owing to his great
love of "peace and good-will," the revenues from this
office were not very large. Usually he tried to act the
part of peacemaker to the parties, and thus prevent a
suit. He officiated at a number of marriages, the parties
sometimes coming many miles to procure his services.

A young couple, from out in the country somewhere,
came to him one evening, and the boys being apprised
of the fact that a wedding was on foot, the news spread,
until the store was crowded to witness the ceremony.
Before leaving, the groom, wishing to pay for the tying
of the knot, gathered from his pocket several small
coins, until he had in all thirty-seven cents, and asked
if that would do. Being assured by the good squire that
it would, the happy pair went on their way rejoicing.

Another store, kept by a nice old lady, supplied the
boys and girls from the schools with cakes, candy, and
nuts. Grandmother Garrison, as we all called her, when
not engaged with customers, was often found seated at
her spinning-wheel, her neat little figure swaying with
the motion of her foot on the treadle, as the wheel sang
its merry tune, and she deftly joined the long pieces of
wool for the yarn, which her busy fingers would knit
into stockings by and by.

What devices the boys resorted to in order to get an
extra trip in the neighborhood of this store. A sudden
misstep, by the help of a friendly weapon, dislodged the
heel of a shoe, which must needs be repaired. A spring
over the fence in the neighborhood of a nail caused a
rent that must at once be taken to the tailor, in accordance with the maxim, "a stitch in time saves nine."

This tailor was a character that must not be overlooked. He was of a very religious turn of mind, and occasionally collected the villagers in the schoolhouse for religious services. Sometimes he was listened to patiently throughout his rather lengthy talk, and then again it happened that by the time his discourse was ended his audience had one by one slipped out, leaving him with a few sympathetic souls. With all his peculiarities, there was not in the neighborhood a more sincerely earnest man in his attempts to do good. What a quantity of water he always seemed to drink! The effect was very funny, when he occasionally held the tin cup, from which he drank, to his lips, and finished a lengthy sentence; the words sounding as if they came from a region far away. Sometimes his meditations interfered with his work, which was usually very well done.

A very small man in the place employed him to make a pair of pants; behold, when finished, they were just long enough to be fastened around his neck! Some of us called him "Samuel, the prophet." He was a dreamer of dreams,—to use his own words, "he had visions." Providence left him a lonely widower, then his visions came thick and fast.

Oh, how many fair women he saw in his dreams! and, oh, dear! to what a persecution was the hapless object subjected for a time. One of these was a visitor at the home of a family who lived in the house now occupied by Mr. Robert Watson, and announcing to some of his friends that his health required a drink from the spring near the house every morning, he never failed, during her stay, to make this pilgrimage.

This same spring of delicious, cool water still refreshes the thirsty traveller, as in days of yore.

Whether he ever found a " pardner," tradition saith not. Like one of his dreams, he vanished from our midst and was lost in the far West.

Something rather embarrassing, and yet very funny to the irreverent members of our little Presbyterian Church, especially the boys and girls, happened as a result of Samuel's zeal, which I must tell you before we leave him. The services in our little church were held, in the summer evenings, before dark, when, in those primitive times, some of the ladies came occasionally with a nice calico dress and a nice sun-bonnet (ladies of means, too), and occasionally a man sauntered in, minus his coat, looking cool and comfortable in his shirt-sleeves. We usually lingered for a chat under the large walnut tree which stands in front of Mr. Reno's house, which was built on the site of the old church. One evening, a young man, who had been in the neighborhood for a short time (and *left town the next day*), had by some means become slightly intoxicated, and strolled into the church-yard. Quite a number of persons were gathered under the shade of the old forest tree, and among them our friend Samuel, who with his usual zeal, which sometimes was without knowledge, took him into the church. We were a little flock, but we had an earnest young minister who labored there for many years, and such voices to lead the singing as one fancies the *angels* have.

While most of them have joined the glorious choir in the " New Jerusalem," there are two of them still in our midst. On this particular evening the words of the opening hymn rose clear and sweet, and were indelibly stamped on the minds of some of the youthful worshippers (?). After the first few words had been sung, the young man aforementioned arose to his feet and, clapping his hands, said, in loud, ringing tones, " Bravo! *first-rate singing!* I've travelled the country all over, and I *never* heard better singing!"

In spite of the young minister's stern *"Be quiet, sir!"* he kept up his applause, until the few quiet words whispered by one of our village doctors persuaded him to go out.

How hard it was to sing properly during such a scene, only those taking part knew.

CHAPTER II.

"The faithful Pastor to his parish dear
  Is like yon elm, that many a rolling year,
Beneath its shade's hereditary reign,
Has heard the gambols of the rustic train:
Whose branches green, that over time prevail,
Have seen the children rise, the father fail:
If counsel sage or bounty he dispense,
He's to his flock another providence.

    *   *   *   *   *   *

Respect his toils, and let your generous care
His modest house, devoid of pomp, prepare.
Within, by virtue's richest treasure graced;
Without, adorned with neat and simplest tastes.
Partake with him the product of thy ground,
And be his altar with thy offerings crowned.
In holy league for mutual good combined,
With his instructions be thy actions joined."

FOR a number of years there was no church building in the Valley, and when the minister could be secured, service was held sometimes in the old log school-house on Division Street and sometimes in the little brick school-house on the property of Mr. Shields.

Rev. Thomas McClelland having preached for a time at the house of Mr. Fisher, and organized the first class in the Valley, preaching sometimes in the house near the old mill and afterwards in the Shields School-House, still later organized the society known as "Hamilton's

54

Class," afterwards the church at Blackburn. Among the names enrolled there was Mrs. Rosannah Brockunier, mother of Rev. Brockunier, who often preached in this neighborhood.

I have in my possession an old class-book marked

"Class-Book for Hamilton's Class: Abraham Laramore, C. L.; Ira Eddy, P. E. Samuel Adams and Jacob Jenks, C. P.'s. Observe the Friday Fasts and live in love. May 3, 1829."

No.	STATE OF GRACE.	MEMBERS' NAMES.	CONDITION OF LIFE.
1	B.	Wm. Trimary.	M.
	B.	Sarah do.	M.
	B.	Samuel Gunsalles.	M.
	B.	Rachel do.	do.
5	B.	Thomas Hamilton.	M.
	B.	Margaret do.	do.
	B.	Rebekah Linn.	M.
	B.	Elizabeth Frazer.	W.
	B.	Jacob Fry.	Wr.
	B.	Jane Merriman.	M.
11	B.	John Boren.	M.
	B.	Elizabeth Boren.	do.
	B.	James Moor.	M.
	B.	Lettice do.	do.
15	B.	Elizabeth Stephens.	M.
	S.	John Glaney.	M.
	B.	Elizabeth Glaney.	do.
	B.	Rosanah Brockunier.	W.
	B.	Archibald Boyd.	M.
20	B.	George do.	S.
	B.	Jane McMichael (removed).	S.
	B.	Abraham Ladamore.	Wr.
	B.	Joseph Gunsalas.	S.
	B.	Luke Gonsalas.	S.
25	B.	Sarah Brockunier.	S.
	S.	James Fry.	M.
	S.	Betsey do.	do.
	B.	Martin Guglinger.	M.
29		Craven Stephens.	

In another class-book for Hamilton's Class, we find
Z. H. Coston, Presiding Elder, and James Wakefield,
Class Leader, with the following members:

No.	State of Grace.	Members' Names.	State of Life.
	B.	James Wakefield.	M.
	B.	Susannah Wakefield.	M.
	B.	Thomas Hamilton.	M.
	B.	Margret Hamilton.	M.
5	B.	Elizabeth Hamilton.	S.
	B.	Margret Hamilton.	S.
	B.	Rebecca Linn.	M.
	B.	Elizabeth Frazer.	W.
	B.	Jacob Fry.	Wr.
10	B.	Jain Merriman.	W.
	B.	John Boren.	M.
	B.	Elizabeth Boren.	M.
	B.	Lettes More.	M.
	B.	Craven Stephens.	M.
15	B.	Elizabeth Stephens.	M.
	B.	Sarah Tanara.	M.
	B.	John Glancy.	M.
	B.	Elizabeth Glancy.	M.
	B.	Rosannah Brockooner.	W.
20	B.	Archibald Boyd.	Wr.
	B.	James Fry.	M.
	B.	Elizabeth Fry.	M.
	B.	Balis Fry.	M.
	B.	Jain Fry.	M.
25	B.	Margret Tinary.	S.
	B.	Feby Waggoner.	M.
	B.	Mary Simereal.	M.
	B.	James Grimes.	M.
	B.	John Stuck.	S.
30	S.	James Brooks.	M.
	S.	Mary Brooks.	M.
	B.	Mary Merriman.	S.
	B.	Elizabeth Grimes.	S.
	B.	Temperance Lustra.	W.
35	S.	William Frazer.	S.
	S.	Ann Linn.	S.

No.	STATE OF GRACE.	MEMBERS' NAMES.	STATE OF LIFE.
	S.	Mary Boyd.	S.
	S.	Mary Stewart.	S.
	B.	Wm. Richey.	S.
40	B.	Jane McDonald.	S.

Among some old certificates of membership of the Hamilton Church are these:

"The bearer, Henry Barnes, was admitted as a Probationer in the Methodist Episcopal Church in Beaver Station on the 20th of October. Since which time there has been no objection to him in that relation, and no doubt but he would have been regularly admitted at the end of six months, but his business required that he should leave the place before the expiration of that term: we therefore recommend him to the attention of our Brethren wherever his lot may be cast, this 22nd day of March, 1834.

JOSHUA MONROE."

"This will certify that the bearer, John Morrow, has been an acceptable member of the Methodist Episcopal Church in Alleghenytown Station.   "D. LIMERICK.

"June 9, 1834."

"The bearer, Nancy Ann Merryman, is an acceptable member of the Methodist Episcopal Church in Liberty Street charge, Pittsburg Station.   "WESLEY KENNEY, S. P.

"October 16, 1836."

The origin of the present Methodist Episcopal Sunday-school was the one opened by Mr. John R. Garrison in the old log church in 1837. His teachers were Isaac M. Cook, Mary C. Way, Martha Mary Nevin, Lizzie S. Olver, Betty Grimes, John B. Champ, Keziah Waters,

Robert P. Nevin, and Samuel Morrow. When the frame building was completed, in which Rev. John White preached in 1839, the school was removed to that place.

In a Sunday-school minute-book kept from August, 1841, to August, 1850, we find many interesting items which show the earnestness and devotion of Mr. Garrison and his assistants. Every Sunday morning, in addition to his Sunday-school work, Mr. Garrison went from house to house, leaving at the door a religious tract, not a house in the village being missed. During the first years of the Sunday-school society, Mr. Garrison was Superintendent; and, although Kenney Goff, Robert Glancy, and others assisted in keeping the "minutes," not until 1844 is there a record of the regular officers, which were Rev. D. Sharp, President; John R. Garrison, Superintendent; Philo Goff, Secretary; Kenney Goff, Librarian; W. Scofield, Treasurer; J. McWilliams, W. Scofield, J. McClelland, B. Gray, Managers.

We cull from the old minute-book the following items:

"AUGUST 1, 1841.

"School opened with singing and prayer by Superintendent, and closed with singing and prayer by Brother B. Gray.

"7 teachers, 45 scholars.

"Cloudy, with signs of rain."

"JANUARY 30, 1842.

"School assembled to-day, but key of the library not being here, the school was dismissed."

"FEBRUARY 13, 1842.

"Cloudy, soft day, with the appearance of rain. Very good behavior in school to-day.

JOHN R. GARRISON.

BRUCE TRACY.

"We generally aim not to let our school last more than one and a half hours.

"7 teachers, 34 scholars."

JUNE 19, 1842.

"A very rainy day. Small school. Few teachers; but pretty well supplied in this respect with visitors. Children addressed by Brother Starr, of the Presbyterian Church.

"3 teachers, 30 scholars."

JULY 31, 1842.

"Had abundance of rain the preceding night; makes it quite cool and comfortable to-day. Quite a scarcity of female teachers.

"4 male teachers, 1 female teacher, 45 scholars."

AUGUST 21, 1842.

"A very pleasant day, but many discouragements; perhaps there is a better day coming; may it be so.

"4 teachers, 41 scholars."

AUGUST 28, 1842.

"B. Gray, one of our teachers, has resigned. A very pleasant day. Tolerable good school.

"3 teachers, 42 scholars."

SEPTEMBER 4, 1842.

"It is now raining.

"3 teachers, 42 scholars."

OCTOBER 16, 1842.

"The Superintendent absent at a quarterly meeting on New Brighton Circuit. A cool, cloudy day, and no fire in the stove on account of not having a stove-pipe."

DECEMBER 25, 1842.

"Our quarterly meeting has been protracted over the three preceding Sundays, in which time there has been a great revival of religion, and some of our scholars have shared in it. A large school to-day and well behaved.

"4 teachers, 37 scholars."

"JANUARY 8, 1843.

"This is the first Sabbath-school since its reorganization.

"At a meeting of the Sabbath-school Society, held January 3, 1843, the following officers were elected for the ensuing year:

"Superintendent, Bro. K. Goff; Secretary, J. P. Kramer; Treasurer, Philo Goff; Librarian, A. Wakefield.

"Managers: Jno. Way, Samuel Peebles, Geo. Rudisill, John R. Garrison, James McWilliams.

"The school is very small to-day, occasioned by the inclement weather.

"6 teachers, 23 scholars."

"JANUARY 22, 1843.

"The weather is fine, and the school tolerably large, but most of our teachers are absent at a protracted meeting at Franklin Meeting House; the librarian is also absent; however, he is excusable, as he has gone to get married.   SEC.

"3 teachers, 47 scholars."

"MARCH 19, 1843.

"Very cold weather. Bro. Baldwin Gray, one of our former teachers, visited the school and took charge of a class.

"4 teachers, 35 scholars."

"MARCH 26, 1843.

"The weather is pleasant and school large. We notice, with pleasure, that Bro. Jno. Way (one of the managers) is present.

"6 teachers, 36 scholars."

"APRIL 10, 1843.

"This is remarkable weather for 10th of April; whilst I am penning this it is snowing, and looks very much like winter. As this is the last day that I expect to meet with the Sabbath school, I do pray the Lord will prosper it as a school, and that superintendent, officers, teachers, and scholars may be so happy as to meet around our Father's kingdom in heaven, where we will praise Him forever, etc., etc.,   Adieu,

"J. P. KRAMER."

WILLIAM RENO.

ROBERT GLANCY.

"MAY 19, 1844.

"A very pleasant morning; quite a large school; no regular male teachers present. I hope the morning air is not cooling the zeal of our eight-o'clock men; the females turn out to a man. The women for perseverance any time before men."

On the last page of the minute-book we find:

"AUGUST 25, 1850.

"A pleasant day; an increase of children and teachers; all went on harmoniously."

In 1839 the first Methodist Church was built at the corner of Broad and Thorn Streets, the site now occupied by the beautiful new edifice, built largely through the munificence of Rev. Charles Thorn. It was built through the efforts of Rev. Charles Thorn, Rev. James Gray, Mr. John Garrison, who for many years was the Sunday-school superintendent, and other zealous Methodists.

Mr. Bruce Tracy, now living at a ripe old age in the house he then occupied, assisted by Mr. Garrison, built the church,—a very neat, comfortable building,—which was removed to Beaver Street a few years ago, and is now occupied by Mrs. Campney (who, with her good parents, often worshipped within its walls) as dwelling and store-room. Within that little church some of the most earnest words that ever fell from the lips of a servant of God were the means of leading multitudes to "the better land."

Rev. John White (father of Judge White) was the first pastor. He was born near Newtown, Frederick County, Va., April 12, 1787, and died in Washington.

Pa., February 23, 1863. His parents were Thomas and Sarah White.

He was about nineteen years old when he commenced preaching in the circuit or district including Winchester and Newtown, then in the Baltimore Conference. He preached in the Sewickley Circuit and lived in Sewickley in 1839–40.

About the year 1857 he purchased the property now owned and occupied by Dr. M. S. Burns, and lived there several years.

I remember hearing him speak at a love-feast, not long before his death, of those early times and some of his after experiences, with such a ring of triumph in his voice that we felt, as we looked at the man who had for so many years "walked with God" and led others to see the beauty of "the narrow way," that he was, like Simeon, just ready to say, "Lord, now lettest thou thy servant depart in peace, for mine eyes have seen thy salvation."

Rev. Joseph Wright, grandfather of Mrs. Dr. McCready of this place, although not resident here, preached alternately with Rev. John White.

His grandfather, Joshua Wright, was one of the early English settlers at Jamestown. He afterwards removed to Washington County, Pa., and cleared a great tract of land. Mrs. Wright, whose maiden name was Harris, belonged to the family from which our State capital received its name.

Joseph Wright, although brought up a Baptist, after his conversion in a Methodist church, began to study for the ministry with a view to joining the Methodist

REV. JOHN WHITE.

Conference. Very few men in his day received so fine an education, and after continued ill-health compelled him to resign his public work as a minister of the Gospel, he devoted much of his time to study.

Mrs. McCready, whose home, after the death of her father, was with her grandfather,—some of whose happiest memories are connected with her life there and the drives to and from school in his company,—tells of the long hours spent in the translation of Latin, Greek, and Hebrew works after the evening worship, in which his clear, sweet voice led the singing, was over and the family had retired, leaving him the quiet hours, often ending with midnight. He was always ready and willing to fill vacant pulpits in the vicinity. The church at "Peter's Creek" was called "Wright's Chapel," for him.

Rev. Charles Thorn, who was largely instrumental in building that first church, is remembered as one who labored zealously for the spread of Methodism and the good of the church at large, helping and encouraging the feeble churches scattered here and there over the country. Thorn Chapel at Glenfield was named for him. Many times he preached from the pulpits of the old churches, and among his last thoughts and wishes and prayers the prosperity of the church here had a large place.

The ground occupied by the Methodist Episcopal chapel, church, and parsonage, and $15,000, were donated by him on condition that the congregation contributed $15,000, so that a new church could be built. The beautiful new church is the result of this bequest.

Mr. Garrison was the Sunday-school Superintendent and Mr. Robert Glancey was Librarian and Secretary.

How many of the "boys and girls grown tall," look back with gratitude to the teachings of Mr. Garrison and the band of earnest workers who labored there. Mr. Gray, Mr. Garrison, and Mr. Reno were among the early class-leaders, men whose houses were always open to the ministerial brethren. Mr. Gray for a time led two classes every Sunday,—one in the little church, the other in the school-house at Shields's.

The church, as was customary at that time, was lighted by candles, the candle-sticks fastened on the walls and posts at the ends of pews. The evening service was announced to commence at "early candle-light," and just as it began to grow dusk, the people went flocking into the church, not so anxious to be sure the candles were really lighted, as many people in all our churches, now-adays, are, to be sure the bell is done ringing before they enter the church, lest they might be a little too early. Here and there over the church some one would start up a familiar hymn, in which all heartily joined. This was continued until the time for the regular service to begin, making the time a regular "*praise-meeting.*" The singing was a feature of the prayer-meetings and protracted meetings, during the winter, that was a *power* for good. There was no choir or organ in those days, but *all* the people sang with a hearty good-will.

The leading members took charge of the lights, to see that they were kept "trimmed and burning." Sometimes they became so absorbed in the sermon that the minister would pause and say, "Will Brother Gray please snuff the candles?" or "Brother Garrison, we would like to have a little more *light.*"

REV. CHARLES THORN.

Mrs. Nancy Way, one of the early Methodists, has a more lasting memorial in the hearts of a grateful people than even the beautiful memorial window in the new church. The sick, the suffering, and the poor were all her friends to be ministered unto. The ministers and their families were all her children, to be thought of and cared for. When the wife of Rev. Sawhill was stricken with small-pox, the whole neighborhood was in terror. Mrs. Way never took a second thought as to her duty in the matter, but with the heroism born of the faith that can remove mountains of danger and difficulty, and the " perfect love that casteth out fear," this widowed mother of a large family, took her post in the sick-room, soothing, comforting, and ministering to the wants of the sufferer. Her quiet, unruffled demeanor, and the sweet, expressive countenance that told of heaven's peace within, inspired patience and trust in the hearts of the afflicted family. When the death angel came, she closed the eyes and folded the hands for the long sleep.

Judge White, who came to Sewickley in 1852, was for more than thirty years the Superintendent of the Sunday-school. His work in this position and in all that concerns the good of the church is felt and acknowledged. His active interest in every new enterprise for the public good is well known. That which comes to me now as a work that will be a lasting monument to his memory, had he done nothing else, is the town-clock, which his energy and liberality placed in the tower of the new Methodist Church. As the spire points us heavenward to the land beyond the clouds, how fitting that our eyes returning to earth should see the hands pointing out the hour, remind-

ing us that the days of probation in which to prepare for
that land beyond time and space are hastening on.   As
the weary watcher in the sick-room waits and hopes for
the morning, each hour that is counted by the clock seems
to say, "be patient; the morning which endeth the pains
and trials of earth, the morning of joy, is at hand."

Rev. Robert F. Hopkins, whose parents came from
England near the close of the seventeenth century, was
born in Bourbon County, Ky., April 16, 1798, and died
in Sewickley, March 3, 1891.   He came to Sewickley in
1849, and built the house lately occupied by Mr. Robert
Watson.   He owned the great tract of land back of the
house, much of which was purchased for the cemetery,
as well as a large portion of the village, which was laid
out in lots by him, and sold for what seems to-day a fabu-
lously low price.

The greater part of his life was spent in connection
with the Pittsburg Conference, and he was Presiding
Elder for nineteen years.   He laid the corner-stone of
the new Methodist Church of Sewickley, and was spared
for several years to worship within its walls.

We quote from the memorial article in the Conference
minutes :—

"The ministry of Brother Hopkins was pre-eminently
itinerant.   Much of it belonged to that period of our
history characterized by very short pastorates and frequent removals.   Some of his fields of labor embraced
vast stretches of territory requiring hundreds of miles
of travel, mostly on horseback, the climbing of mountains, threading of forests, swimming of swollen streams,
and lodging in rude cabins.   That was the 'heroic age'

REV. ROBERT HOPKINS.

of Methodism west of the Allegheny Mountains; and of the heroes, none were more heroic than Robert Hopkins. He well earned the large place he holds in the respect and affections of his brethren in the ministry and of the people whom he served."

He was married, November 14, 1833, to Miss Pamelia Scott, of Brooke County, Va. There were born to them five children,—two sons and three daughters. Three of these have passed to the spirit world, leaving one son, Prof. Hamline Hopkins, of Ypsilante, Mich., and Mrs. Mary Lipp, of Sewickley. Nature was generous in giving our brother an exceptionally fine physique. He was fully six feet in height, squarely built, and as straight as a rule. He was of commanding presence and noble bearing, had a keen eye, was always courtly in his manners, but exceedingly affable. He was the very soul of honor, despising all that savored of littleness or meanness.

He was one of the comparatively few men who succeed in keeping the heart young. The children in the Sunday-school always smiled when they saw him coming into the room, for he was sure to go around among the classes and speak some kind words to them. He rarely passed a child on the street without exchanging a few pleasant words. As a preacher, Robert Hopkins was a workman that needed not to be ashamed. Whether dealing with philosophical or practical truth, he seemed equally at home. His style was lucid, logical, and manly. He held his subject well in hand, always making out what he undertook. He laid no claim to what is called the "witchery of oratory," but his discourse bristled with points well taken and admirably put, and often spiced

with sparkling wit and humor, so that he easily held
the attention of young and old. His last sermon was
preached in Sewickley Church about a year before his
death. He sat in a chair while delivering his discourse,
which was full of interest and profit, and will long be
remembered by those who heard it.

A few months before his death he was brought to the
church, and from his chair made a short talk to the
Sunday-school. He remained for the public service, at
the close of which he pronounced the benediction. It
was a day of joy to the old veteran, and his last spent
in the house of God on earth.

The following have been the preachers of Sewickley
Methodist Episcopal Church :

1839. John White and Joseph Wright.
1840. Joshua Monroe and J. White.
1841. P. McGowan and H. McCall.
1842. H. McCall.
1843. D. Sharp and J. Houston.
1844. D. Sharp and W. P. Blackburn.
1845. W. Long and J. W. Baker.
1846–47. J. L. Williams.
1848. B. F. Sawhill.
1849. J. K. Miller.
1850. T. Cronage and B. F. Sawhill.
1851. R. Hopkins and Joseph Horner.
1852. A. G. Williams and W. P. Blackburn.
1853. T. P. Sadler and J. Pollock.
1854. H. D. Fisher and A. E. Ward.
1855. L. R. Beacom and S. Burt.
1856. L. R. Beacom and F. D. Fast.
1857. J. C. Brown and George Crooks.
1858. D. A. McCready.
1859. D. A. McCready (Sewickley a station).

BUILT 1854.

M. E. CHURCHES.

BUILT 1839

1860–61. H. W. Baker.
1862–63. S. G. Kennedy.
1864–66. W. H. Locke.
1867–68. Joseph Horner.
1869–71. C. A. Holmes.
1872–74. J. R. Mills.
1875–76. A. L. Petty.
1877–78. W. B. Watkins.
1879–81. William Lynch.
1882–84. M. J. Sleppy.
1885–86. W. J. Miles.
1887–88. L. H. Woodring.
1889–90. J. S. Brackin.
1891–92. H. L. Chapman.

LEAVING THE OLD CHURCH.

The last services in the old brick church, which was to be taken down to make room for the present edifice, were held September 18, 1881.

The bell rang at the usual time for Sunday-school. The hymns, "In the morn of life," and "Jesus is calling for thee," were sung, and prayer offered by the Pastor, Rev. Wm. Lynch. After some time spent with the regular lesson, the Assistant Superintendent, Mr. John Johnston, read a letter from the absent Superintendent, Judge White, written in London, telling of the notable things he had seen; this was followed by a talk from Father Hopkins, telling something of his early life. After singing "Welcome to glory," the school was dismissed, to meet the next Sunday in Choral Hall.

At the eleven o'clock morning service, the Pastor preached a missionary sermon from Luke xii. 48. At the beginning of the service six children were baptized,—

Harry S. Lake, Ora R. Lake, Sarah Lake, George A. Roe, Olive B. Little, and James V. Brush.

The choir was composed of Mr. John Rosensteel, Leader; Miss Bell Roe, Organist; F. R. Peters, J. B. Ague, James McDonald, W. W. Rosensteel, William Young, Hattie Gaston, Ida McDonough, Kittie Erwin, and Lizzie Stuck.

At the evening service, the anthem, " Praise the Lord," and the hymn, " Waiting, only waiting," were sung. The sermon was from Eph. i. 13, 14; hymn 445, the Doxology and benediction, followed by the anthem, " How beautiful upon the mountains," closed the solemn and interesting services.

The chapel of the new church was dedicated November 20, 1881. The morning sermon was by Rev. Mr. Locke; text, " What mean ye by these stones?" Rev. Robert Hopkins and the Pastor read alternately the One Hundred and Twenty-second Psalm. Mr. Hopkins dedicated the church. Anthems, " Oh, how Beautiful," " How Lovely is Zion," " Deal Gently, O My Father."

In the afternoon, the sermon, from Forty-eighth Psalm, twelfth and thirteenth verses, was by Rev. W. B. Watkins. Prayers were offered by Rev. W. L. Wallace, of the U. P. Church, and Dr. James Allison. The anthem, " The Lord Reigneth," was sung.

In the evening the sermon was by Mr. Locke, from Luke xviii. 2. Appropriate hymns were sung and prayers offered.

Laying of corner-stone of new M. E. Church. Services were commenced in the chapel at two P.M., July 25, 1882. After the anthem, " How Beautiful are Thy

M. E. CHURCH.

BUILT 1884.

Dwellings," had been sung and Scripture reading by the Pastor, Rev. Wm. Lynch, there was prayer by Rev. McGuire and the singing of appropriate hymns, followed by the reading of a history of Methodism in Sewickley by Judge White. Addresses were delivered by Revs. Wakefield, McCready, and Holmes, former pastors.

A large glass jar, which was to be put under the corner-stone, was packed in the study by Judge White, Ralph Johnston, John Patton, and Robert Glancy. It was sealed by John Patton, who, after the services in the chapel, carried it to the corner, where services were held. After prayer, singing, and reading of church Discipline and appropriate selections from the Scriptures, " Father Hopkins" read a list of the contents of the jar, which he then deposited with the help of William Dickson, the contractor. The stone bears the inscription, " Laid July 25, 1882." The jar contained a Bible, hymn-book, copy of the *Christian Advocate*, copy of each of the daily papers, a history of Methodism in Sewickley, the names of all the members of the Church, the names of teachers and scholars of the Sunday-school.

Then followed reading from Discipline, "In the name of Father, Son, and Holy Ghost," by Father Hopkins. Singing, by congregation, hymn 316. Prayer by Dr. Holmes. Gloria Patria, led by Judge White, and Benediction by Father Hopkins. Ministers present were, Revs. Hopkins, Lynch, Boyle, Wakefield, McCready, Holmes, Horner, McGuire, Hull, Ellis, and Peters of the Methodist Church, and Dr. Bittinger of the Presbyterian, Dr. Camp of the Episcopal, and Rev. Cole, African M. E. Church, Sewickley. A social meeting was held in the evening in the chapel, at which Father Hopkins and Judge White related some incidents of the early days of Methodism in Sewickley.

Of the young men of the M. E. Church, Sewickley, who became ministers, is Rev. Frank R. Peters, whose mother resides on Fife Street. He was born in Moon Township, Allegheny County. When five years old he came to Sewickley. He was educated in the Sewickley public school, McKeesport Academy, and Mount Union College. He taught school for a time, commencing when but sixteen years old. In 1883 he was married to Miss Lizzie Anderson, of Sewickley. He is now pastor of the M. E. Church at Mahoningtown, Pa.

Rev. A. C. Ellis was born in Detroit, Michigan, in 1851, and in infancy was removed to Sewickley. He was educated in the Sewickley public schools, Allegheny College, and Drew Theological Seminary. He was married, in 1885, to Miss Delia McMunn, of Ohio. He is now pastor of the Smithfield Street M. E. Church of Pittsburg, Pa.

Rev. John F. Murray, brother of Dr. R. J. Murray, was born at Blackburn, near Sewickley, in 1854. He was a pupil of the public school at Blackburn, afterwards attending Sewickley Academy and Allegheny College previous to entering the senior class of Ohio Wesleyan University, from which he graduated in 1877. He was licensed to preach at Blackburn Quarterly Conference, held at Mount Sewickley camp grounds. In 1878 he was married to Miss Luanna Brush, of Ohio. In 1883 he entered the Boston school of theology. He is now pastor of the M. E. Church at Wilkinsburgh.

HON. J. W. F. WHITE.

JOHN N. WHITE, ESQ.

Rev. Samuel M. Mackey was born in Londonderry, Ireland, and came to Sewickley in his early boyhood. He was educated in the Sewickley public schools and Allegheny College. He is now pastor of Simpson M. E. Chapel, Liberty Street, Allegheny City, Pa.

Rev. George S. Holmes, son of Rev. C. A. Holmes, D.D., of the Arch Street M. E. Church, Allegheny, who was for a time a resident here, was born in Steubenville, Ohio, February 9, 1854. He commenced his school-life in the Third Ward Pittsburg public school, and was a pupil of the Iowa Wesleyan University during the time his father was president of that institution. He received the degree of A. M. from the Western University of Pennsylvania in 1882. He studied law in Harrisburg, while in the office of Hon. M. S. Quay. While pursuing his law studies, he had such a longing to preach the Gospel, that he commenced the study of theology with his father, and, when just ready to be admitted to the bar, was received into the Pittsburg Conference of the M. E. Church in 1881. He is now pastor of the M. E. Church at Scottdale, Pa.

Rev. James M. Thoburn, Jr., was born at St. Clairsville, Ohio, June 23, 1856. He was educated at Allegheny College, Meadville, Pa. Part of his boyhood was spent in Sewickley, where he is kindly and affectionately remembered. He was a missionary to India four years, pastor of the English Church at Calcutta, except the last eight months of his stay, when he was pastor of Union Chapel, at Simla, the headquarters of the English government in the Himalaya Mountains. He is now pastor of the M. E. Church at Oil City, Pa.

June 14, 1882, he was married at Corry, Pa., to Miss Emma F. Merchant.

Rev. William Bruce Ringley was born in Sewickley, June, 1857, and died at the age of twenty-eight years, having spent all his life in the Valley and among the people he loved. He received his early education at the public school, and was a member of the first class to graduate from that institution in 1876. After attending Mr. Way's Academy for some time, he spent two years teaching in the little school by the water-works, during which time he made a lasting impression on the minds and hearts of his pupils. His next step was to enter the Polytechnic Institute in Allegheny as a pupil, and his death occurred shortly before the time he expected to graduate. He was a great student, and had he lived would have made his mark in the world. Two years before his death he was licensed to preach the Gospel, and many times preached in Allegheny, Bellevue, Glenfield, Bridgewater, and his own dear Sewickley. Those who had been associated with him in church and Sunday-school in all his relations of assistant superintendent, treasurer, teacher, and class-leader rejoiced when, from the pulpit of their own church, his gentle voice was heard telling the " wondrous story" of redeeming love, and pleading with sinners to accept as their friend the Saviour that was his constant companion.

Mr. Ringley often expressed the feeling that to him life's journey would be very short, and in consequence of this ever-present feeling was all the more zealous and eager to work. He was a dear lover of Nature, and we feel that he realizes now fully the meaning of these words:

JOHN JOHNSTON.

B. C. CHRISTY, ESQ.

"There everlasting spring abides,
And never withering flowers."

A beautiful and touching tribute of love and respect
to the memory of their friend was the service of prayer
and song held by the side of his grave every Sunday
evening during the summer after his death. At the
young people's prayer-meeting held just before service
on Sunday evenings, the following hymn, composed by
their friend " Willie," was often sung to a familiar tune :

I'm but a traveller through this desert of tears,
I'm but a traveller through this desert of tears;
I'll journey along for a few more years,
And then I'll see the promised land.
        Glory to Jesus, His name I'll praise
        While time is for me, and thro' endless days
        I'll praise Him in the glory land.

I once lived in Egypt in bondage to sin,
I once lived in Egypt in bondage to sin,
Then Jesus in His mercy found out me,
And, glory to His name, I'm free.

I'm walking with Jesus hand in hand,
I'm walking with Jesus hand in hand,
On the high brow of Nebo soon with Him I'll stand,
And He'll show me all fair Canaan's land.

There, there are mansions bright, fair to see,
There, there are mansions bright, fair to see,
And Jesus my Saviour has builded them for me,
In the city of the great, great King.

Death's dark river, oh, why should I fear?
Death's dark river, oh, why should I fear,
While Jesus at the helm my bark will steer
And moor me on the golden shore?

                                        W. B. RINGLEY.

Rev. Charles Edward Locke was born in Pittsburg, September 9, 1858. During his father's pastorate in Sewickley he left an impress on the minds of his play-fellows, some of whom remember his preaching to them after spending a little time in his father's study as he rehearsed his sermons. He graduated in the class of 1880 from Allegheny College, Meadville. In December, 1882, he married Miss Mina J. Wood, daughter of Captain John A. Wood, of Pittsburg. Mr. Locke is now pastor of the Taylor Avenue M. E. Church at Portland, Oregon.

Rev. H. L. Chapman, D.D., the present pastor, was born March 24, 1832, at Stoystown, Somerset County, Pa. He was converted during a protracted meeting held in Blairsville, Pa., at the age of fourteen, at which time he united with the Methodist Episcopal Church. He was led, through the influence of Rev. John Coil, the Presiding Elder of the Pittsburg Conference, to begin his public work as a minister of the Gospel at the early age of nineteen years. In July, 1853, he was married to Miss Agnes C. Stahl, of Ligonier, Pa.

Dr. Chapman has had some of the best charges in the Conference, having spent the five years previous to his coming to Sewickley at Johnstown, sharing with his people all the horrors of the dreadful flood, giving his prayers and sympathy to the afflicted, and seeking by word and influence to encourage and lift up the discouraged and cast down. The degree of A.M. was received from Allegheny College in 1861, and that of D.D. from Mount Union College, Ohio, in 1880.

When the call came for the nine-months' men in 1862,

REV. H. L. CHAPMAN, D.D.

and so many responded to the call, going forth to all the untried realities of the dreadful war, subject to many trials and temptations, Dr. Chapman went out as Chaplain for the 123d Regiment.

For four years he filled the position of Presiding Elder of the Allegheny District. In addition to his pulpit and pastoral duties, Dr. Chapman takes a great interest in the young people's meetings, usually filling the position of President of the Epworth League. He came to Sewickley in the autumn of 1891.

The singing in the Methodist Episcopal Church has been led for eighteen years by Mr. John A. Rosensteel, sometimes as precentor, and at other times leader of a choir. Mr. Rosensteel is well known in Sewickley, and many other cities and towns, as a musician. He married Miss Mary Glancy, daughter of Mr. Robert Glancy, of Sewickley. They reside on Thorn Street.

The Sunday-school connected with the Methodist Episcopal Church, which was started by John R. Garrison in 1837, is now the largest Sunday-school in Sewickley, having an enrolment of three hundred and seventy-five scholars. The Superintendents have been John R. Garrison, Kinney Goff, Judge White, D. N. White, John Johnston, B. C. Christy, and John N. White. Mr. White, the present Superintendent, has filled the position for ten years. He was born at the old homestead at the corner of Chestnut and Broad Streets, and has grown up in the Sunday-school, successively filling the positions of pupil, teacher, and superintendent, as well as positions of trust connected with the church. He was married in 1886 to Miss Julia French, of Fort

7

Wayne, Indiana. Mr. White is a well-known lawyer in Pittsburg; his residence is on Broad Street, near Thorn.

The infant class, which has been under the superintendence of Mrs. R. M. Irwin (formerly Mrs. T. C. Little) for the past twenty-three years, assisted by Mrs. Daniel Dé Linn (formerly Miss Jennie Johnston) for ten years, and, owing to an increase of pupils, also by Miss Ella Ward for the past two years, owes its origin to Mrs. Judge White. When Mrs. White went to the Sunday-school the first Sunday spent in Sewickley, she proposed to gather up the little ones and form an infant class. The old frame church was then used as a Sunday-school room, but had not yet been divided into rooms, so, when told there was no room for an infant class, Mrs. White said, "I will find a place." My informant, who was then a pupil in one of the larger classes, says she fancies she can see the little flock, led by Mrs. White, going around to Broad Street, to the tailor shop owned by Mr. Samuel Morrow, which occupied the site of the present parsonage. There the good work began which has grown to the present large infant class. Besides a large number of classes in the main room, there are two Bible classes, taught by Judge White and Mr. J. P. Baily, the well-known architect.

The first Presbyterian minister known to have preached in the Valley was Rev. John McClain, who was pastor of Montour's church across the river. He preached in barns, private houses, or in the woods from 1802 to 1808.

The first mention of a regularly organized church at Sewickley is in the church records of 1808. Mr. Andrew McDonald was pastor part of his time until

JOHN A. ROSENSTEEL.

1818. During the interval between 1818 and 1822, when the church was again organized, Rev. Francis Herron, D.D., and Rev. Elisha P. Swift, D.D., preached here a number of times.

The first church was a log-house built in 1818. Services had been held for a time in the woods, sometimes in a sort of shed in the "Oak Grove" of Mrs. Beers, and at last a lease of the grove was secured for forty years and the log church built. It was on the property owned by the late Robert Watson. The first sermon preached in that building was by Rev. Michael Law, pastor of Montour's church.

The members of the church organized in 1822 were James McLaughlin and Thomas Backhouse, Elders; private members, Nancy McLaughlin, William McLaughlin, Mary McLaughlin, Sarah Backhouse, Mrs. Mann, Thomas Waggoner and wife, Jane Lester, and Jane Vance. Rev. Mr. Andrews, who was engaged to preach for one-third of his time, was promised $35.50. From 1831, when Mr. Andrews's labors ceased here, the people were indebted to Rev. S. C. Jennings and others for occasional preaching.

The next reorganization was in 1838. The names of members were Alexander Ingram, James S. McComb, John B. Champ, James McLaughlin, George Flower, Thomas Waggoner, Mary Ingram, Ellen Ingram, Margaret Nevin, Ann McComb, Eleanor Orr, Margaret McComb, Mary Olver, Jane M. Flower, Mary Smith, Eliza Campbell, Mary P. Johnston, Nancy McLaughlin, Jemima Anderson, Isabella Waggoner.

Dr. S. C. Jennings, who was appointed by Presby-

tery to preach in Sewickley Valley as missionary ground,
deserves especial mention. Although not a resident of
the Valley at that time, he was identified with much of
the early religious history of this place. Three of his
daughters, Misses Emma, Zelia, and Mary, reside on
Fleming Avenue, and his son, S. D. Jennings, M.D.,
a practising physician in our borough, and an earnest
church worker in the Presbyterian Church, lives at the
corner of Beaver and Walnut Streets, his house occu-
pying the spot where the log-house of John Hoey, son
of Thomas Hoey, stood. Rev. S. C. Jennings was born
in Burgettstown, Washington County, Pa., in 1803. He
was a son of Dr. Ebenezer Jennings, a physician, and
a member of the Legislature to represent Washington
County at Lancaster in 1806. His grandfather was a
minister and physician, who was a surgeon in the army
of the Revolution and the first Moderator of the Synod
of Pittsburg, in 1802. During his labors in Sewickley
Dr. Jennings frequently preached in the Shields' school-
house, and there, in infancy, Mary Anderson, afterwards
wife of Rev. James Allison, was baptized by him. He
became a student of medicine, that his life might more
nearly resemble that of his Master, "who went about
doing good," healing the body and speaking words of life
to the sin-sick soul. In his "Recollections of Seventy
Years," he says, in speaking of his work in Temperance-
ville, where he lived, and in addition to his work as
editor of *The Christian Herald* (now *The Presbyterian
Banner*, edited by Dr. Allison) preaching and pastoral
work for the two congregations at Sharon and Mount
Pisgah,—

BUILT 1818.

"About twenty years I was constrained to yield to the application of persons who needed help, having as my chief compensation the satisfaction of purchasing the medicine and relieving suffering humanity. . . . This mode of life afforded an opportunity of doing good to some people who could not have been reached by any one merely a minister."

Dettmer Basse, maternal great-grandfather of Dr. S. D. Jennings, was a Westphalian by birth, and minister to France from Frankfort, then a free city; he came from Paris in 1801 and settled in Conequenessing Valley, where he purchased ten thousand acres of land.

Philip Louis Passavant (whose family left France in 1594 on account of religious persecution) was born in Frankfort-on-the-Main; he married in 1807 and settled in Zelianople. One of his daughters, Emma Marie Wilhelmina Passavant, married Rev. S. C. Jennings. Her brother, Rev. William A. Passavant, is a well-known and beloved pastor, whose work for the sick and suffering in the hospitals, as well as his daily devoted Christian life and example, is so well known and felt. Zelianople was named by Mr. Basse for his daughter Zelia, mother of Mrs. Jennings and Dr. Passavant.

The second Presbyterian Church building, which occupied the site of the residence of Mr. Reno, just across the street from the present house of worship, was built in 1840.

Rev. Daniel E. Nevin, the first pastor, had been preaching for two years in the school-room of Edgeworth Seminary, where the church was organized. The first time Mr. Nevin preached in the Valley, there being no steamboat running that day, he walked from Allegheny.

Rev. D. E. Nevin was born at Shippensburg, Pa., graduated at Jefferson College in 1833, entered upon the study of law in the office of the late Richard Biddle, but in a short time became a student of the Western Theological Seminary in Allegheny, and graduated in 1836.

After a few years of faithful earnest work in the infant church here and the church at Fairmount which shared his time and labors, throat trouble, brought on from exposure to a severe rain-storm when returning from a church service, caused him to give up both charges, much regretted by his parishioners. Having taken charge some time previously of the Edgeworth Seminary, the Sewickley people had the comfort of seeing and worshipping still with him; but the Fairmount congregation were inconsolable at his loss, saying, " We would rather have you, if you were only able to sit in the pulpit, than any other minister." His gentle, quiet manner endeared him to teachers and pupils, but ill health compelled him to abandon this work, too. During the subsequent years of retirement and literary work, he always seemed like the beloved disciple, and his life a sermon from the text, " Little children, love one another."

When Mr. Nevin was locating here, having accepted the charges of Fairmount and Sewickley, he was advised by a friend to take up his abode out at Fairmount, as Sewickley would never be much of a place.

Rev. James Allison was chosen pastor in 1848. The Sewickley Church was his first charge, and he brought to the work all the ardor and enthusiasm of a young minister realizing his high calling and the open door of opportunity in this fair Valley. A Bible class during the

REV. D. E. NEVIN.

week, and a class for the study of the Shorter Catechism on Sunday afternoons, in addition to prayer-meeting and Sunday-school work, were as powerful agents for good as his sermons every Sunday. Quite a large number of persons united with the church during his pastorate from 1848 to 1863. The first sermon I ever remember to have heard was from his lips, and as the years sped on and the prayer-meeting became a place of interest, the pastor's remarks, the earnest prayers of the faithful few who were never absent, as well as the "Songs of Zion" sung by loved voices, made an impression that has been a help and inspiration "all along the years." Rev. James Allison was born in Pittsburg in 1823, but was brought up near Bakerstown under the ministry of Rev. John Moore and Rev. Leland R. McAboy. He graduated from Jefferson College in 1845. The same year he entered the Western Theological Seminary in Allegheny, and graduated in May, 1848. The next Sabbath he preached his first sermon in Sewickley. He had arranged to go to Iowa, and was quite taken by surprise when asked to remain as stated supply for one year. In October, 1849, he was ordained and installed pastor. The congregation, though small, was much scattered, and the pastor's duties were sometimes arduous. During his pastorate there were received into the church five hundred and eight persons. The pastoral relation was dissolved at the request of Dr. Allison that he might become one of the editors of the *Presbyterian Banner*. Dr. Allison resides in our borough, and his face is often seen and his voice heard in the churches of the different denominations.

Dr. J. B. Bittinger was chosen pastor when the pulpit became vacant on account of the resignation of Dr. Allison because of ill health. For twenty-one years he was the devoted, dearly-loved friend as well as pastor of a congregation that, even when physical weakness prevented his being able to minister in the sanctuary, refused to have the bond between pastor and people sundered. We cull from a sketch by Mr. John Way, Jr., one of his elders and a most devoted friend, the following words:

"Joseph Baugher Bittinger was one of a family of twelve, the offspring of German parentage. He was born March 30, 1823, at his father's farm, about three miles north of the town of Hanover, York County, Pa. At the age of twenty-one, Dr. Bittinger was graduated from Pennsylvania College, Gettysburg. Five years later, completing his theological studies at Andover Seminary, he was licensed to preach the Gospel, having spent part of the time meanwhile in teaching a private school in his native place. For one year, 1849–50, he was principal of the Abbott Female Seminary at Andover, Mass. He was then chosen professor of rhetoric and philosophy in Middlebury College, Vermont. This position he filled two years, during which (in 1851) he married Miss Catherine Forney, a young lady of Hanover, Pa. In 1852 he was ordained an evangelist at Cornwall, Vermont. About this time he was chosen pastor of the newly-formed congregation of the Euclid Avenue Presbyterian Church of Cleveland (installed in 1853), and remained until 1862. For the next two years, being disabled by rheumatism, he did little work. Recovering somewhat, he accepted a call to the Sewickley Presbyterian Church in May, 1864, and was formally installed in July. Constrained by continued ill health, he tendered his resignation as pastor of the church, February, 1885. It was reluctantly and tearfully accepted, but, at the request of the Session, the formal dissolution of the pastoral relation was not consummated, and

REV. JAMES ALLISON, D.D.

the man beloved by all died in the arms of his people in the early morning of April 15, 1885.

"Dr. Bittinger believed in the worship of work. Mere sentiment in religion, without some practical, tangible evidence of the hope that is within, found in him but little sympathy. With a clear and intensely logical mind stored with knowledge far out-reaching his profession as a minister of the Gospel, Dr. Bittinger had a command of language and a facility of illustration which was marvellous. For many years he never wrote his sermons, and, indeed, made no previous preparations for the utterance of his thoughts. For his illustrations he trusted to the inspiration of the moment, and they were always brilliant and to the point. A marked instance of his wonderful power in extempore speaking was manifested in an address on Martin Luther which he delivered by invitation before the Presbytery of Allegheny, at the Central Presbyterian Church, Allegheny City, in November, 1883, on the occasion of the four hundredth anniversary of Luther's birth. In the preparation of this address, which occupied nearly two hours in its delivery, no pen had been put to paper. Taken down by a skilled phonographer, and afterwards published in pamphlet form, it is a piece of polished rhetoric and unanswerable logic.

"Dr. Bittinger's gifts were all of a high order. If in any one direction he excelled, it was as a teacher. He was, indeed, a teacher of teachers. His aptness of illustration came in here especially. Nor was he satisfied with his ability to illustrate; he was ever filling his mind with new facts, drawn from his personal observation and from his extensive reading. Principles and methods of teaching were a constant study, and the teachers of Allegheny County owe more to him, perhaps, than to any other man, for original and fundamental ideas on this point."

From Miss Bittinger's "Memorials" of her father, we quote these words, written by his brother:

"During those twenty years on the banks of the Ohio, which from his study in the morning sun was ever before his eye, he

had many temptations to go into what would be deemed larger
fields and more inviting lines of work; but, knowing that he had
the unqualified confidence of his people, I doubt if he ever seri-
ously entertained the thought of leaving them.   The field is
always large enough; it is the man that is wanting.   These
temptations were to other churches, to chairs in colleges and
seminaries, amongst them to the presidency of Washington and
Jefferson College, Pennsylvania. Mr. Blaine's Alma Mater, to which
he was urged by all the influence of his mother church.   And to
take away every impediment in his path, a college classmate of
large ideas and a generous heart stepped forward and promised
the endowment of the presidency in the sum of forty thousand
dollars: But to all these inducements he preferred his quiet
church by the river, and the ceaseless shuttle went to and fro.
Gradually, as the floods in the river abraded the banks along its
sweeping tide, carrying it out into the vast ocean, so his own life
was flooding out into eternity.

"His study was his workshop, with a most select assortment
of intellectual tools and appliances, all for use, nothing for ornament, except a few choice pictures and bronzes, notably that of
the great Reformer.   And here, as he rhymed it in his poem,
'The Weaver,' published in the *Atlantic Monthly*, the shuttle
went ever back and forth, at the fearful cost of life-blood."

THE WEAVER.

BY J. B. BITTINGER.

I.

The weaver sat by his burden,
    Waiting the work to begin,
Dreamily throwing the shuttle
    Backward and forward between;
Questioning much of the pattern,
    Watching for it to be seen.

PRESBYTERIAN CHURCH.
BUILT 1840.

The shuttle was filled with colors
  Of every shade and glow;
Thoughtless he scattered their radiance,
  Falling above and below,
The pulse of the loom ever beating
  Solemnly to and fro.

The throb of the loom grew stronger,
  The shuttle flew faster between.
One thread seemed a line of shadow,
  Another a ray serene;
But the solemn loom wove together
  Equally shade and sheen.

The weaver sat by his burden,
  Watching the low-setting sun,
Wearily throwing the shuttle,
  Ending as he had begun;
Pondering still of the pattern—
  The pattern that was done.

II.

The weaver took to his bosom
  The web as it fell from the loom;
In its many folds lay hidden
  Whatever of light or gloom
Had come through the flying shuttle,
  From the gray of dawn till doom.

Buttercups with dew besprent,
  Forget-me-nots in tears,
Bedight the fabric of the loom
  Through all the dawning years:
The texture of those morning hours
  A fairy weft appears.

Lilies with their vestal light,
  And orange blossoms pale,
Illume the woof of youthful days
  And show a bridal veil—
'Mid blue-eyed flax and ears of wheat,
  A distaff and a flail.

Patterns of the after years,
  The olive and the vine,
Adorn the richness of the folds,
  Its costliest threads entwine;
And through the labors of those days
  Altars and firesides shine.

Barren husks from winter fields,
  And tardy asters' light,
Glint o'er the few remaining threads
  That dimmed the weaver's sight;
And then a shadow falls upon
  The web, and, lo! 'tis night.

The following words, written by Thomas Patterson, Esq., one of his elders, express very beautifully the character of this great scholar, devoted pastor, and humble Christian:

When I am dead, and men shall come
To lay me in my last, long home,
Could I by chance hear what they say,
Awe-struck and whispering round my clay,
    What words would bear the sweetest tone?

I shall not care what art hath done,
I shall not care for trophies won;
For art, with sense, shall pass away
    When I am dead;

REV. J. B. BITTINGER, D.D.

But that, perhaps, one might be there
Could say, " He brought me strength to bear
My trial, brought me truth and light
In darkness, strove he for the right :
I think God hath him in His care,
    Now he is dead.

Rev. W. O. Campbell, D.D., the present pastor, was born in Middlesex Township, Butler County, in 1841, and shortly afterwards removed to the town of Butler. He attended Witherspoon Institute. In 1858 he entered Jefferson College, and graduated in 1862. In August of the same year he enlisted in the United States Army, Company K, 134th Regiment, Pennsylvania Volunteers, Colonel M. S. Quay. After the battle of Fredericksburg he was promoted to the captaincy of his company. Mr. Campbell entered the Western Theological Seminary in the fall of 1863, then, after two years spent at Princeton Seminary, was licensed to preach by the Presbytery of Allegheny (now Butler) in 1865, and preached three years at Depere, Wisconsin. He was married September 14, 1868, to Miss Mary L. Shaw, of Glenshaw, Pennsylvania. In 1870 he was called to Monongahela City.

For two years, 1883 and 1884, he taught in the department of homiletics in the Western Theological Seminary. In 1885 the degree of D.D. was conferred by Wooster University. Dr. Campbell was installed pastor of Beaver Street Presbyterian Church, Sewickley, September 8, 1885.

One who for many months was deprived of the privileges of God's house, whose days of weariness and pain

were cheered and blessed by the faithful ministrations of
her pastor, always associated him with her idea of "the
disciple whom Jesus loved;" and, with this in mind, the
following quotation from a sermon delivered soon after
taking charge of this flock, seems especially appropriate:
"'By this shall all men know that ye are my disciples,
if ye have love one to another.'

"The grace which was most manifest in Christ was
that which the Apostle Paul calls the greatest of all
graces. The strength of the Church is in its unity, and
its unity is in the spirit of love, which is the bond of
perfectness. Christ prays for His people that 'they all
may be perfected into one; that the world may know
that thou didst send me, and lovedst them, even as thou
lovedst me.'

"The most powerful testimony for Christ which disciples can give is, not that in which the intellectual ele-
ment predominates, but that in which the spirit of love
and gentleness and compassion is most clearly manifest.
That which drew publicans and sinners to Christ was His
love. It is a striking fact, that those who were regarded
as the worst people were strongly attracted to one who
was the truest, the holiest, the most just of the sons of
men; but it was not His truth or His holiness or His
justice that first attracted them; it was His love. The
secret of His power was in His all-embracing love.
This, dear friends, is the spirit that we want, and just as
we have it may we expect to be efficient witnesses for
Christ. What, then, is necessary that we should fulfil
our vocation? What is necessary that this church
should in the future be a power for good in the midst

REV. W. O. CAMPBELL, D.D.

of this community? It is not necessary that it should have an eloquent ministry; it is not necessary that it should be strong in point of intellect, or wealth, or numbers. If we are satisfied to build up a church which shall have the power that resides in these things, we shall not be powerful in the sense that Christ desires us to be. I believe that the temptation to self-complacency for our sacrifices, our devotedness, our self-denial, to glory in ministers, in means, in numbers and contributions, is very powerful. Let us look to the Lord to deliver us from this snare. Let us try to look at such success as this implies as altogether external. True power depends on other conditions. Christ did not call many wise; He did not seek the wealthy as such; He did not count the number of His disciples. That is a morbid disposition which manifests itself in 'counting heads.' What Christ seeks in a church is spiritual power.

"We want intellect, indeed, but intellect that shall be wholly sanctified by the Spirit of God; we want wealth, but wealth that shall be in the hands of those who shall be willing to devote it to the extension of the Redeemer's kingdom: we want numbers, but numbers of such as shall be saved.

"We want, for the purpose of bearing testimony to a callous world, a people who shall live in daily union with Christ, who shall be filled with His spirit, who shall be strong in faith, who shall be steadfast in the ways of righteousness, who shall be willing to accept the lowliest work in the service of Christ, whose hearts shall be full of love to their Lord and Master."

The Fiftieth Anniversary exercises of the Presbyterian Church, on February 17, 1888, were exceedingly interesting.

The exercises were:

ANTHEM—*"We Praise Thee, O God."*
BY THE CHOIR.

HYMN 32—*"All Hail the Power of Jesus' Name."*
BY CONGREGATION.

READING OF THE SCRIPTURE.

PRAYER.

TRIO—*"Lord, Thy Glory Fills the Heavens."*
MRS. J. SHARPE M'DONALD.
MR. W. W. WHITESELL. MR. ROBERT J. CUNNINGHAM.

1863–1864—*Historical Address.*
REV. JAMES ALLISON, D.D.
SOLO.
MRS. J. SHARPE M'DONALD.

1864–1888—*Historical Addresses.*
MR. JOHN F. ROBINSON, MR. GEORGE H. CHRISTY.

ANTHEM—*"It is a Good Thing to Give Thanks."*
CHOIR.
THE SABBATH-SCHOOL.
MR. THOMAS PATTERSON, MR. FRANK C. OSBURN.

HYMN 369—*"Oh, Where are Kings and Empires Now?"*
CONGREGATION.
DOXOLOGY.

BENEDICTION.

SOCIAL MEETING.

The elders who have served in this congregation are: James McLaughlin, John B. Champ, Thomas Back-

FIRST PRESBYTERIAN CHURCH.

house, Robert Anderson, James Laird, William Woods, M.D., George H. Starr, Campbell McLaughlin, Samuel R. Williams, John K. Wilson, Theodore H. Nevin, Robert H. Davis, William P. Jones, John K. Wilson, James L. Carnaghan, John Way, Jr., John Irwin, Jr., John F. Robinson, Melancthon W. McMillan, George H. Christy, W. W. Waters, Thomas Patterson, Frank C. Osburn.

Theodore Hugh Nevin was born October 23, 1815, near the village of Roxbury, Franklin County, Pa., about ten miles from Shippensburg. When six years old the family removed to Shippensburg, where he attended school until he was sixteen years old. He then went to Pittsburg and studied with his brother Daniel, their brother John W. Nevin being the instructor. After three years spent in study he went to Michigan to engage in mercantile pursuits, returning in two years to Pittsburg. His business career extended over fifty years of faithful, earnest work. He lived in Sewickley during the last thirty years of his life, and during all that time was an earnest Christian worker, an elder in the Presbyterian Church, teacher of a Bible-class, and for many years superintendent of the Sunday-school. As a member of his Bible-class and a regular attendant of the weekly prayer-meeting, where he was *always* found, I recall many of his earnest words. Mr. Nevin first became officially connected with the Western Theological Seminary of Allegheny in 1842, when he was elected treasurer of the endowment fund. At an alumni meeting of the faculty, directors, trustees, and friends of the Seminary held in the First Presbyterian

Church of Pittsburg shortly before his death, the following resolution was adopted :

"To our worthy and esteemed treasurer, Theodore H. Nevin, Esq., who, with very small compensation, has managed the finances of our Alma Mater with such admirable skill, for now more than forty years, that not one dollar has been lost by injudicious investment or otherwise, we tender not only our congratulations and the thanks of the friends of the institution, but our heart-felt sympathy in his present affliction and prayers for his speedy recovery."

Mr. Nevin became connected with the Western Penitentiary in 1864, and was an earnest, active worker for the good of the inmates. He was one of the leaders in securing the abolishment of solitary confinement there, and many times appointed as a delegate to important meetings in Cincinnati, St. Louis, New York, London, etc. When the war broke out, no one in the Valley did more to help and encourage the soldiers. He aided largely in organizing the Nevin's Battery (Battery H), of which the late Colonel John I. Nevin was captain. He gave his elder son to his country, who was soon called to give up his young life for the cause.

In every movement for the public good in Sewickley,— the water-works, the new cemetery, the improvement of the roads, etc.,—Mr. Nevin took an active part ; but his warmest sympathies and most earnest work were given to the beloved Church which owes so much to him.

Mr. Nevin was married in 1844 to Miss Hannah Irwin, sister of Mrs. Daniel Nevin and Mr. John Irwin, of the Valley.

Mr. Charles F. Nevin, who succeeded his father in

WILLIAM WOODS, M.D

GEORGE H. STARR.

the lead business in Allegheny, is well known to all our citizens. He married Miss Lizzie Grafton. They, with their two children, Theodore and Elizabeth, reside on Academy Avenue, near Quaker Valley Station.

Of the young men who have become ministers of the Gospel who were connected with the Presbyterian Church and Sunday-school were:

Rev. Thomas Beer, born in Sewickley and baptized in the "Old Sewickley Church."

Rev. Isaac M. Cook, born in Ohio, and, while attending Sewickley Academy, united with the church here.

Rev. John M. Peebles, who was for a time a medical student, but afterwards became a minister.

Charles B. McClay, a pupil of the old Academy at Quaker Valley, was a pastor several years, afterwards a physician and poet.

Rev. A. M. Reid, Ph.D., of Steubenville, was born in Beaver County, Pa.; a teacher and student in Mr. Travelli's Academy, studied theology, and became a successful pastor, and Principal of Steubenville Female Seminary.

Rev. W. W. Ralston united with the church while attending Mr. Travelli's Academy, and afterwards studied theology, and has filled important charges in Ohio and this State.

Rev. John Quincy Adams Fullerton spent his boyhood in connection with this church, and is now pastor of the Presbyterian Church, Apollo, Pa.

Mr. Robert Cochran, a Sewickley boy, and a pupil of the Presbyterian Sunday-school, is now pastor of a large and flourishing congregation in Harrisburg, Pa.

Of the first three Sunday-school superintendents, Mr.
Allison, Prof. A. M. Reid, and Mr. Starr, who in turn
served for a short time, I remember nothing, Sunday-
schools had been held at different places, but the first one
connected directly with the church was started by Mr.
Allison in 1848. There were four teachers, Mr. and Mrs.
Starr, Prof. Reid (now Dr. Reid, of Steubenville), and
Mr. John Way (now of New Lisbon, Ohio). The next
superintendent, who filled the position for many years,
was the Principal of the Academy. Every Sunday morning he went from class to class, shaking hands with the
teachers, speaking a kind word, or gently stroking the
head of one and another of the children, while his face
beamed with love and good will to all. He used to give
us some of the most helpful and instructive talks about
his previous life as a missionary. I remember a sermon
he preached on influence, from the text, " No man liveth
unto himself;" and if ever a minister practised what he
preached, it was Rev. Joseph S. Travelli. After his work
in the Academy was finished, leaving its impress on hundreds who are to-day scattered throughout the length and
breadth of our land, other duties and cares were taken up,
for which the days seemed all too short, but he never in the
midst of his busy life lost sight of his " boys and girls."
Even when his work at Riverside among the erring and
depraved took so much of his time and energy (a work
that made a good impression on the minds of many who
afterwards led reformed and useful lives), he found time
to visit the sick and speak a word of comfort to the dying.
Who can estimate the harvest of his life-work as missionary, teacher, Sunday-school superintendent, and *friend?*

THEODORE H. NEVIN.

ROBERT H. DAVIS.

The weekly prayer-meeting held in the little church was well attended, and all parties and meetings of a social nature were arranged so as not to interfere with Wednesday night. By the light of a lantern, plodding our way through the mud, sometimes stopping to take up an overshoe that had been left behind, and again escaping some of the mud by climbing a fence and going through a grassy field, we reached the meeting, where all our tribulations by the way were forgotten, and we had "a foretaste of heaven." There were not many in the small congregation who were willing to take part in conducting the meetings, but among the few who did were two who never allowed fatigue or a press of business in store or workshop to prevent their being ready at the appointed hour to go to the place of prayer. One of them, a perfect Nathanael in his guileless life, impressing others in his quaint remarks with the reality and beauty of his religion; the other, whose humble words of adoration and praise kindled the zeal and strengthened the faith of many a weak disciple, and whose quiet deeds of charity and kindness caused many to "rise up and call him blessed:" these two, obeying the commands of their Master as they ministered to "the necessities of the saints," were united by the bond of Christian love and sympathy. As I remember them lingering by the way-side at the close of the meeting, ere going to their homes, earnestly conversing of the things "unseen and eternal," I fancy them now, in the "home beyond," recounting the way in which they were led, and uniting in the "New Song" as they rejoice over every soul gathered home from this loved spot.

The elders we remember as serving in those early days were Dr. Woods and Mr. Starr,—faithful, earnest, devoted, godly men, the influence of whose example is still felt in our midst.

Rev. David McKinney, D.D., Editor of the *Presbyterian Banner*, was long a resident here, and many times preached in both the old and new churches. For many years after he had grown old and feeble and partially deaf, he occupied the chair, near the pulpit of the new church, which had been presented by the members of the congregation as a token of love and gratitude.

Oh, how many precious memories cluster around the dear old church! Mrs. Starr beautifully expressed these thoughts in the following lines:

THOUGHTS ON LEAVING THE OLD CHURCH.

BY MRS. RACHEL HOOKER STARR.

O Thou whose uncreated mind
    Fills all the boundless realms of space,
By time, by distance not confined,
    Eternity thy dwelling-place!

Thou, Lord, earth's corner-stone didst lay
    When morning stars together sung;
This earth, these heavens, will pass away,
    Thy power endures—forever young.

But what is man, frail child of dust!
    Age follows age like wave on wave;
One moment gives him life at first,
    Another brings him to the grave.

W. W. WATERS.

The works of art men proudly build
   Endure but a few fleeting years ;
Our lives, still shorter, sooner filled,
   Our earth a vale of sighs and tears.

Here mourn we dear, departed friends
   Who shouted as *this temple* rose :
Their works of faith and love remain,
   While they are wrapped in calm repose.

They to these walls impart a breath,
   And, hark ! what is the spirit sound ?
"Oh, be thou faithful unto death,
   And thou shalt be in glory crowned."

Honored and consecrated spot,
   To memory thou wilt still be dear ;
Accept the tribute of the heart,
   The parting sigh, the falling tear !

Oh, may the Heavenly Dove still rest
   With the first guardian of this fold,
And be his crown, in regions blest,
   Richly adorned with gems untold.

O Father, Son, and Holy Ghost,
   Thou One in Three and Three in One,
Help Thou the watchman of our host
   To blow the trump with certain sound.

On him may grace most plenteous fall
   As he on Zion's faithful waits,
That crowds may, at Salvation's call,
   Tread joyful the new temple gates.

Mr. Way says that the first intimation of a Sunday-school among the early records is an item in which "one dollar's worth of Sunday-school tracts" is charged. This was in 1829, and the Sunday-school started then in the old log church continued until 1835. It was held during the summer, Mr. James McLaughlin and Mr. Hodge conducting the school. Among the teachers were Mr. Vance, Miss Eliza Anderson, Miss Polly Beer, Miss Mary McLaughlin, and Mr. William Grossman.

The teachers we remember as connected with the school during the years when Mr. Travelli was Superintendent were Mr. and Mrs. George H. Starr, Messrs. John Way, Jr., T. H. Nevin, James M. Loughridge, Misses Rebecca L. Way, Mary Anderson, Sarah Lambert, Lizzie Jones, Amelia Nettler; then, later on, Mary Woolridge, Henry M. Atwood, Kate Wilson, Rebecca Wilson, Belle Wardrop, Mary Wardrop, Susan M. Ellis, Daisy Davis, Mattie Nevin, Jennie Davis, Rebecca Davis, Margaret Porter, Emily Neely, Agnes L. Ellis.

The Superintendent of the Sunday-school at the present time is Mr. W. W. Waters, manager of the Presbyterian Book-store, Pittsburg. Mr. Waters was born in Allegheny County, is of English descent, and grandson of a Revolutionary soldier. Mrs. Waters is a daughter of the late Rev. B. C. Critchlow, of New Brighton, Pa. Mr. Waters is a faithful church-worker, both as elder and Sunday-school superintendent.

Mr. George H. Christy, one of our elders, has a large Bible-class, which he has taught very faithfully and acceptably for twenty-five years. The class is comprised of both ladies and gentlemen, who esteem it a privilege

LEETSDALE PRESBYTERIAN CHURCH.

to listen from week to week to Mr. Christy's faithful, well-prepared teachings.

Mr. John Way, Jr., has been teaching since 1849. He commenced when a pupil of the Academy, and in that time has had under his care three hundred and eighty-nine young men. Outside of this number, a great number of young men have, through the quiet work—the harvest of which we cannot estimate—of Mr. Way and his working pupils, been influenced and helped by a little note sent or a good book lent, thus "coming into contact with the spirit of the Bible-class."

Five of the young men of that class have become ministers,—Andrew C. Ellis and Samuel Mackey uniting with the Methodist Church, W. J. Radir joining the Episcopal, John A. Duff connecting with the United Presbyterian, and Robert Cochran uniting with the Presbyterian Church of Sewickley.

Mrs. Way (formerly Miss Kate Wilson) was for many years a faithful, earnest teacher, and she still feels the same deep interest in "her boys," although they have left her care and are scattered here and there, many of them owing the ability to "choose the good and forsake the evil way" to the influence and prayers of the faithful teacher, so gratefully remembered. Rev. J. Q. A. Fullerton was a member of her class.

The infant class is taught by Mr. George W. Cochran, who has held the position for twenty years. Mr. Cochran was married to Miss Martha Nevin, daughter of the late Rev. D. E. Nevin.

Captain Cochran, as he is usually called, has filled many positions of trust in the borough,—burgess and councilman, besides being one of the water commissioners and a director of the Sewickley Cemetery. To his energy and influence we owe the fire department, the engine-house being named for him.

The mission school at Osburn is connected with this church; it was organized about twenty-six years ago through the efforts of Miss R. B. Davis (now Mrs. Dr. Willard). Mr. William McKown was the first superintendent. Among the teachers were Miss R. B. Davis, Miss Haslin, Mr. James, and Benjamin Parks.

For a time the school was conducted in the old schoolhouse, but at length the present commodious building was planned by Mrs. R. H. Davis, who, being laid aside by ill health, committed the work to her brother, Captain George W. Cochran, who carried the work forward to completion. The superintendents have been, Mr. William McKown, Mr. Baldwin, Mr. Wm. Jones, Mr. Bakewell, and Judge Over.

The Leetsdale Presbyterian Church was organized August 1, 1864, in Edgeworth Seminary, with forty-three members, all of whom had been dismissed by certificate from the Borough Presbyterian Church.

Dr. Allison, in his historical discourse, says, "Edgeworth Seminary opened its hospitable doors to the Leetsdale Church as it had done to the Sewickley Church, and public worship was held there until the building was consumed by fire in February, 1865; after that services were held for a time in the 'Shields' school-house,' on the high ground above the Beaver Road on this side of Little Sewickley, where a weekly prayer-meeting had been maintained for many years."

REV. R. S. VAN CLEVE.

Sewickley Church, at the beginning of the present organization, was largely indebted to a woman; but Leetsdale is under still greater obligations to a woman.

Mrs. Eliza Shields was the daughter of a Revolutionary soldier who had served on the staff of General Washington. From her father she had inherited large possessions here, and for years it had been in her heart to erect to the memory of her father, Major Daniel Leet, and her mother, Wilhelmina, something that would be a blessing to her children and her children's children and her neighbors, and also to the glory of God. Now her time had come; and, although far advanced in life, she acted with great vigor and intense earnestness. First she donated a lot estimated to be worth $1200; during the summer she put up a chapel at a cost of $2300; then she erected the beautiful house of worship now occupied by the Leetsdale Church at a cost of $18,000. The chapel was dedicated to the worship of God in the summer of 1865. The corner-stone of the church was laid June 23, 1868, and it was dedicated to the worship of the triune God on Sabbath, November 14, 1869. The dedication sermon was preached by Rev. James Allison. The sermon in the afternoon was by the Rev. David R. Kerr, D.D., of the United Presbyterian Church, and in the evening by Rev. S. J. Wilson, D.D. In the meantime the people had erected a manse, which, with the lot, cost $4000, and furnished the church at an expense of $1500; and afterwards a son of Mrs. Shields, namesake of her father, Daniel Leet Shields, made a bequest of $5000, the income of which is forever to be expended in keeping the church buildings and grounds in good repair.

Mrs. Shields died March 21, 1872, and her works will follow her throughout all generations. Though dead, she will through the church which she builded preach the Gospel during all the succeeding ages.

On the 8th of March, 1865, Rev. W. W. Eels was called to the Leetsdale Church, but on June 23, 1866, ill health caused him to give up the charge to which he had ministered for a time.

Rev. James Platt was installed pastor in June, 1867, and resigned August, 1867.

Rev. R. S. Van Cleve was called to the pastorate of Leetsdale Church January, 1870, and installed in May. He resigned September 21, 1886, leaving the beloved people he had served so long, in the hope of regaining by rest and retirement the health whose failure caused him to resign; his last sermon was October 3, 1886. Mr. Van Cleve is a native of Beaver Meadow, Carbon County, Pa. He is at present pastor of the Chestnut Street Presbyterian Church of Erie, Pa. Through the efforts of Mr. Van Cleve and his people, "Van Cleve Chapel" was built, where Rev. Mr. Sayres, a returned South American missionary, labored as pastor.

Rev. Edgar F. Johnson, who succeeded Mr. Van Cleve, was born at New Jackson, Ohio, January 19, 1859. He graduated from Amherst College 1885, and from the Western Theological Seminary 1887. He was installed pastor of the Leetsdale congregation July 12, 1887, and resigned his charge March 25, 1890.

Rev. James L. Reed, the present pastor, was born in Washington County, Pa., and spent his boyhood on a farm. He was educated at Washington and Prince-

REV. JAMES L. REED.

ton Colleges, graduating from the latter in 1870. He studied theology in the Western Theological Seminary of Allegheny. His first charge was at Independence, Washington Presbytery, where he remained eight years. He next spent one year in missionary work at Puebla, Colorado, after which he took charge of the church at Barnesville, Ohio, remaining six years. In July, 1891, he was installed pastor of the Leetsdale Church.

During the past two years about $7000 have been expended by the Leetsdale congregation for a new organ and other improvements.

Mr. William Abercrombie, the leader of the congregational singing, has been for many years a resident of the borough.

Mr. John K. Wilson, who was an elder in the Presbyterian Church on Beaver Street, was one of those who united to form the Leetsdale congregation. He was born in Washington, Pa.; graduated at Washington College in the class of 1815. He removed to Sewickley in 1851. He died at Leetsdale, July 4, 1882. Dr. Allison says of him: "He was an intelligent, painstaking, and thoroughly conscientious man in all the relations of life. He was a diligent student of the Bible, watchful of his own heart and ways, well informed concerning the progress of the church, intensely anxious for its welfare and for the suppression of evil in every form. His prayers were exceedingly rich in appropriate quotations of Scripture, and in earnestness and tenderness; none who heard them will ever forget them."

Mr. Jacob Guy came to Sewickley many years ago. How clearly I remember his earnest prayers in the prayer-meeting in the old brick church during the pastorate of Dr. Allison. He is remembered in the Leetsdale Church as an earnest, devoted, faithful man of God.

The elders who have served in the Leetsdale Church are: John K. Wilson, Jacob Guy, Henry M. Atwood, Robert Wardrop, clerk and treasurer of Session; William Seaman, James M. Kerr. Mr. Wilson and Mr. Guy having previously served as elders were the choice of the people when the organization took place, and the others are the members of the present Session. The church membership is one hundred and thirty-nine. The Sunday-school, under the superintendence of Mr. Seaman, numbers one hundred and twenty scholars.

Mr. Way, in his address on the "Olden time in Sewickley," says: "In 1826, David Shields, for the use of his neighbors and tenantry, built the little brick school-house still standing on the high ground near to and opposite his late residence.

"This building was used for school, prayer-meetings, and general church purposes. On November 27 of the same year Mr. Samuel Shannon opened there a small day-school. From time to time, as occasion offered, there was preaching there and prayer-meetings; the itinerant preacher always finding at Mr. Shields's house a welcome for himself and his horse. In this little school-house on the hill, about the year 1835, Mrs. Shields began an afternoon Sunday-school, which she personally superintended many years.

"The school began usually as soon as the spring weather would admit, and continued always to Christmas, when each boy and girl received some suitable

WILLIAM ABERCROMBIE.

present at the hands of the 'elect lady,' and a bountiful supply of cakes and apples. At times, these cheerful entertainments were held in her own house.

"This Sunday-school continued without intermission, except during the winter months, until about 1841, during which time Mrs. Shields received occasional assistance in the superintendence from John B. Champ and Isaac M. Cook. Her teachers were the members of her own household and of one or two neighboring and intimate families, and sometimes the lady teachers of the Edgeworth Female Seminary.

"One of her aids deserves especial mention, her carriage driver, a giant African of brawn and muscle, who could neither read nor write, and whose knowledge of mathematics was limited to four,—the number of horses in his farm team. At times, when Mrs. Shields was unable from rheumatism to climb the steep hillside to her little Sunday-school, big Harry Robinson would tenderly assist her with his huge arms. He used his one talent, strength, in a good cause and with a loving heart.

> " 'I think the lesson is as good
>   To-day as it was then;
> As good to us called Christians,
>   As to the heathen men,—
>
> " 'The lesson of St. Christopher,
>   Who spent his strength for others,
> And saved his soul by working hard
>   To help and save his brothers.'

"In 1859, Mrs. Shields' Sunday-school was resumed

under the care of Mr. John K. Wilson, and in 1864 it became a part of the Leetsdale Presbyterian Church, so continuing up to the present time."

ST. STEPHEN'S EPISCOPAL CHURCH.

The origin of the congregation that worships in the neat little church (an interior view of which we give on another page) was on this wise. When General Cass was about to build a summer residence at Osburn, (the home now occupied by Mr. Thomas Hare,) to those who urged him to take up his abode there permanently, his objection was based on the fact that there was no Episcopal Church in Sewickley. Mr. Colhoun, whose residence was near Park Place Hotel, or what was then the Sewickley Academy, urged General Cass to unite with him in trying to found a church here, although there were not many Episcopalians in the Valley. Mr. Frank Hutchinson, who was engaged in business in Sewickley, united with General Cass and Mr. Colhoun in their efforts, and soon the present church building was the result.

Rev. Joseph P. Taylor, Rector of Kenwood school for boys, in New Brighton, Pa., held two services in Sewickley in 1861, baptizing one child, Adelaide Colhoun. His report led to the engagement of P. Ten Broeck, Deacon, of Pittsburg, to hold services three Sundays a month for six months from December 21, 1862. The services were held in the Methodist Church the first Sunday. The congregation consisted of eleven persons.

The small brick Presbyterian Church was offered and

SHIELDS' SCHOOL-HOUSE.

BUILT 1826

accepted, and the work was carried on until Sewickley was appointed a station by the Board of Missions. Then Rev. Ten Broeck devoted the whole of his time to the parish.

At that time (1863) a threatened invasion of the State caused much excitement, and, as soon as it died away, Mr. Ten Broeck and Mr. George Colhoun began to solicit subscriptions for the purchase of a lot which Mr. Colhoun held for that purpose. Rev. Mr. Ten Broeck prepared plans and specifications, and broke the ground, September 28, 1863. The corner-stone was laid by Rev. David Cook Page, D.D., of Allegheny City, assisted by other clergy in the vicinity. The church was occupied for the first time, March 4, 1864, and consecrated May 28, 1864, by Rt. Rev. Alonzo Potter, D.D., Bishop of Pennsylvania, assisted by Rt. Rev. Wm. B. Stevens, D.D., (who preached the sermon,) and seventeen clergy.

General Cass, Mr. Colhoun, and Mr. Hutchinson purchased the remainder of the lot, corner of Broad and Vine Streets, upon which a parsonage was built.

August 16, 1865, Rev. William P. Ten Broeck resigned the charge of St. Stephen's, and on September 1 officiated for the last time.

October 1, 1865, Rev. William Wilson officiated for the first. He resigned in 1868.

Rev. Samuel Earp took charge January, 1869, resigning November, 1870.

S. B. Moore was called January, 1871; resigned in 1873. He was succeeded by Rev. George W. Easter, who resigned in 1876.

Rev. Norman W. Camp, D.D., of the diocese of Long Island, N. Y., took charge January 1, 1877; resigned November 20, 1882.

December, 1882, Rev. Edmund Burke became pastor, and remained until 1885.

The present pastor, Rev. Robert A. Benton, "comes of a New England family, which has been established in Connecticut and Massachusetts since the earliest settlement of the country. His boyhood and youth were spent in North Carolina, where his father had the care of a small parish. From thence he went to Trinity College, Hartford, Conn., from which he was graduated in 1864. Mr. Benton at once engaged in teaching, being connected with St. Paul's School, Concord, N. H., for twenty years. While there he studied theology, and was ordained to the ministry in 1869, after which he added missionary and parish work to his duties as a teacher. In 1884 he removed to Meadville, Pa., and in April, 1885, to Sewickley, in order to take charge of St. Stephen's parish.

"Though making parish work the chief thing, Mr. Benton has not laid aside the *rôle* of teacher, having taught for four years in Mr. Way's Academy, and, after that, having organized the grammar school," which he now conducts so successfully.

The first church baptism in St. Stephen's was that of Mary Jane Helyar, July 24, 1863, by Rev. William P. Ten Broeck.

The first class confirmed by Bishop Kerfoot, November 17, 1865, consisted of George W. Cass, George Francis Colhoun, Francis Helyar, Mrs. Mary Ann

INTERIOR OF ST. STEPHEN'S EPISCOPAL CHURCH.

Akin, Miss Martha E. Colhoun, Miss Mary R. Cass, and Miss Julia W. Schweppe.

The first marriage of any of the church members was that of Francis M. Hutchinson and Miss Sophia L. Cass, by Rev. William P. Ten Broeck, February 8, 1866. Mrs. Hutchinson is the only one of the members who composed the new congregation in 1863 that is left in Sewickley.

MEMORIALS.

There have been from time to time memorials presented to the church of St. Stephen's by its parishioners.

One set of books, consisting of a large Bible and two prayer-books, was presented by the friends of the deceased mother of the first rector, Rev. William P. Ten Broeck, February 26, 1864. " Blessed are the dead who die in the Lord."

In 1864, the silver communion service was presented by Mr. George W. Colhoun, " in loving memory of his aunts, Martha and Ann Colhoun."

For Christmas, 1881, a fine cabinet organ, bearing the inscription, " In loving memory of our mother," was the gift of Messrs. John and Frank M. Hutchinson.

White embroidered hangings for lectern and pulpit were the gift of Miss Lucy Little. White embroidered altar cover from Miss Elizabeth Cass.

At Easter, 1887, the original altar was replaced by one of quartered oak, bearing the inscription, " To the glory of God, and in loving memory of our sister, Mary Little. Entered into rest, March 12, 1886." The gift of Mrs. William Gorman, Mrs. H. A. Gilmore, Miss Lucy Little, and Mrs. E. L. Mudie.

The altar service-book was given by General George W. Cass.

The bishop's chair was presented by the Misses Cass.

The brass altar cross and retable bear the inscription, "To the glory of God, and in loving memory of Mary Louise Hutchinson," and were from Miss Violet Cass.

The brass altar vases are "In memory of my brother, George Dawson Cass," from Mrs. Frank M. Hutchinson.

In 1890 a credence shelf was added to the chancel furnishment, "In loving memory of Mary Louise Hutchinson," by her mother, Mrs. Frank M. Hutchinson.

On Christmas, 1891, a beautiful font of pure white Italian marble was presented to the church by David Morris Smith, Irvin H. Smith, and Frank B. Smith, Jr., children of Mr. and Mrs. Frank B. Smith, members of St. Stephen's. The words, "In the Name of the Father, and of the Son, and of the Holy Ghost," are carved upon it.

Mrs. Hepburns Johns made and presented a font cover of oak and brass, containing the words, "One faith, one Lord, one baptism."

The following are the names of the ladies of the Chancel Society of St. Stephen's Church: Miss Rose Davis, Miss Carrie Davis, Miss Virginia R. Chaplin, Miss Nellie Hutchinson, Miss Lizzie Richardson, Miss Mamie Dippold, Mrs. Robert J. Cunningham, Mrs. Percy L. Rider, Mrs. George P. Rose, Mrs. Frank B. Smith, Mrs. James Ritchie, Mrs. Joseph P. Rankin, Miss Minnie Anderson, Miss Elsie Graff.

REV. ROBERT BENTON.

Associate Members.—Miss Jane McDonald, Miss Maggie McDonald.

President.—Miss Virginia R. Chaplin.

Vice-President.—Mrs. Frank B. Smith.

Treasurer.—Miss Rose Davis.

Secretary.—Mrs. George P. Rose.

Vestrymen.—Mr. B. W. Doyle, Mr. Percy L. Rider, Mr. James R. Gilmore, Mr. Harry W. Richardson, Mr. Frank B. Smith, Mr. Edward B. Taylor.

The first minister of any denomination who held regular religious services in Sewickley Valley was Rev. Francis Reno, an Episcopal clergyman, who began his work as early as 1798. The original name was Ré Nault.

Two brothers, William and Philip Ré Nault, fled from France to find in the new world a refuge from religious persecution. They first settled in Virginia. Rev. Francis Reno, whose name had become in some way changed from the original, was a descendant of William Ré Nault, and had Indian as well as French blood in his veins, William Ré Nault having married a young Indian girl.

The names of those who subscribed to pay his salary, either in money or grain, were John Bean, John Way, John Griffith, William Leet, James Fletcher, William McGlachlin, Joseph Olver, John Vail, John Stairs, William Larimore, Samuel Thomas Olver, James Hutchinson, Hannah Heigus, William Cheny, Patrick Bolden, Jeremiah Wright, Solomon Vail, David Vail, George Harris, Samuel English, Benjamin Gunsalas, Joseph Fisher, John Olver, Hugh Larimore, John Bales, Sr.,

Christian Martin, Jessie Fisher, Samuel Merriman, Frederick Merriman, Samuel Smith, H. Lee, Henry Ulery, Adam Patterson, and William Sutton.

The place of preaching was in Squire Way's barn, which stood near the spot where Mr. Walker lives.

Mr. Reno preached until 1810, giving one-third of his time. It is said that many of his descendants live in Beaver County; and we have one of them here in the person of Mr. Elias Reno, who lives at Edgeworth.

ST. JAMES'S ROMAN CATHOLIC CHURCH.

The few families of the Roman Catholic faith in the borough and vicinity being anxious for a church home in the Valley, Father Reed, pastor of Beaver Church, came to the cottage of Mr. Creighton, on the "Shields's nursery grounds," once a month, on a week-day, for two years and held service.

After Mr. Creighton's removal to the old Garrison property in the borough, service was held there for another two years.

A lot was bought on Walnut Street in 1860, and paid by the five families who composed the congregation, and a subscription-list started for a building fund.

Father Reed's field embraced a large territory, now embracing nine parishes. He travelled on horseback, was well acquainted, and was very successful in making converts and gaining the co-operation of other individuals outside of his own church, and securing their help. Owing to the failing health of Father Reed, and finally his death, the church was ministered to by the German Fathers of St. Mary's, Allegheny; and then,

ST. JAMES'S ROMAN CATHOLIC CHURCH.

for about two years, by the Passionist Fathers of the South-side. The first regular pastor was Rev. J. D. Swickert, who was assisted by Rev. J. Kunkle. The next pastor was Rev. Coyne, succeeded by Rev. Kaylor.

Rev. F. F. O'Shea, the present pastor, was born west of Killarney, that historic spot in Ireland, near the birth-place of the famous Daniel O'Connell, in 1863. He came to the United States of America in 1873; was educated in the public schools of New England, and afterwards studied rhetoric, philosophy, and theology under the tutorship of the Franciscan Fathers, who are affiliated with St. Isidore's, in Rome. He is a devoted, earnest pastor, and also an earnest advocate and helper in every effort for the good of the community. The congregation now consists of about five hundred souls. The first church building was a small frame structure. A brick building succeeded this, but soon after its completion the roof fell in, and it had to be rebuilt. The present building is a large brick edifice, beautifully decorated inside. A large new pastoral residence has lately been built.

The church of St. James has a large flourishing Sabbath-school connected with it, also the following societies: "The Sodality of the Blessed Virgin," the "Catholic Benevolent Legion," and the "League of the Sacred Heart of Jesus."

UNITED PRESBYTERIAN CHURCH.

There were in Sewickley a few families which, before taking up their abode here, had some of them in Pittsburg the acknowledged centre of the United Presbyterian body in the "States;" others away off in Scotland and Ireland, been members or adherents of the United Presbyterian Church.

As a longing for the church of their forefathers grew and strengthened, the question began to be agitated as to the advisability of making an effort to establish a church here. A committee waited upon Dr. J. T. Pressly (of blessed memory), at his home in Allegheny, in the spring of 1863, consisting of Prof. T. E. Wakeham and Mr. Robert Dickson, to seek his approval in view of the proposed undertaking. Prof. Wakeham, now a resident of the borough, was at that time a resident of Allegheny, an elder in the Third U. P. Church, and secretary of the board of church extension, of which Dr. Pressly was president. He is a well-known educator in Pittsburg and Allegheny; was for a time Principal of Sewickley Academy and Sewickley public school.

Dr. Pressly warmly approved of the undertaking, so a meeting was held at the home of Mr. John Thompson, at which there were present, Mrs. A. W. Black and Messrs. William Miller, Alexander McElwain, James Ellis, John Thompson, Robert Dickson, W. A. Ellis, and James Park, when resolutions were adopted, a subscription list started, and six hundred dollars subscribed towards the fund for a church. A lot was purchased on Broad Street, and liberal hearts and willing hands carried the work forward.

Dr. Pressly came and preached, with a view to organizing a congregation, on August 2. The Methodist brethren kindly offered the use of their church, which

REV. W. A. McKENZIE.

JOHN THOMPSON.

PROF. THOMAS E. WAKEHAM.

ROBERT DICKSON.

ALEXANDER McELWAIN.

JAMES ELLIS.

FRANK McCLELLAND.

12

WILLIAM MILLER.

was used by the little band until their own church was built. On the evening of May 4, 1864, after having had preaching by supplies every two weeks during the winter, twenty-two names were enrolled as a nucleus for the new congregation, Dr. Pressly preaching and conducting the organization.

The new church was dedicated June 12, 1864. Dr. Pressly, conducting the services, preached the morning sermon from Psalm cxxvii. 1; Dr. J. B. Clark, in the afternoon, from Psalm cxix. 106, and Rev. Mr. Locke, of the Methodist Church, closed the interesting services by a sermon in the evening from the words found in Luke xiii. 6, 7. All day the house was filled by an attentive audience.

The elders chosen were James Ellis and William Watt, men whose lives were a beautiful commentary on the Gospel they professed. Though long since gone from the church here to join the blood-bought throng in the temple not made with hands, they are still held in loving remembrance in the hearts of many who worship here, and by others who have providentially been led into other paths, and in new fields of labor serve the Lord.

The first break in the little band of worshippers was caused by the death of Mr. Alexander McElwain soon after the completion of the church building. Gentle, loving, and kind, his earnest voice, as we heard it in the cottage prayer-meetings which were such a comfort and delight, seems to echo in the walls of memory to-day.

A Sabbath-school was organized with Mr. John Thompson as Superintendent.

Among the teachers we remember Mrs. McCleery, Miss McElwain, Mrs. Reed, Miss Black, Miss Thompson, Messrs. Alexander McElwain, Frank McClelland, James J. Ellis, and William and James Watt.

Two of the boys from that Sabbath-school are ministers in their own denomination.

Mr. William A. Miller was born in Sewickley in 1865; was educated in Sewickley public school, Western University, and Allegheny U. P. Theological Seminary. He was married, June, 1893, to Miss Blanche Patterson; is now pastor of Stowe congregation, Cleveland Presbytery, Ohio.

William E. Stewart was born in Beaver County and educated at Westminster College.

Rev. W. A. McKenzie, the first pastor, was called in 1865. This was his first charge, which he accepted full of zeal for church work and the principles of the United Presbyterian Church. He resigned this charge in 1871, and has since that time been pastor of the church at Salem, N. Y.

Rev. D. S. Kennedy was the next pastor, called in 1872. He filled the pulpit for six years, and resigned to accept a call to Somonauk, Ill.

W. L. Wallace, D.D., the third pastor, was born in Pittsburg, August 23, 1834. His preparatory course of study was received at Cannonsburg, and he graduated from Jefferson College, Cannonsburg, Pa., in 1857. He studied theology at the United Presbyterian Seminary of Allegheny. His first charge was at Newville, Pa. He entered upon his pastoral duties there in the autumn of 1861. The following May he was married to Miss

REV. W. L. WALLACE, D.D.

REV. A. G. WALLACE, D.D.

Elizabeth Riddle, of Allegheny. Dr. Wallace accepted the call to the Sewickley Church June, 1879, and was the dearly loved pastor and friend of his congregation until continued ill health caused him, July, 1886, to resign.

"He was a good man, full of the Holy Ghost and of faith," and his failing health seemed to draw the hearts of his people more closely to him, so that the tie between pastor and people was severed with *deep, heart-felt regret.* Seeming to rally somewhat, he accepted the position of President of the College for Freedmen at Norfolk, Va.; but after laboring there two years he was obliged to relinquish the work, as it was evident that the sound of the Master's footsteps, as He came to call His faithful servant, would soon be heard. He died at Asbury Park, N. J., where he had gone for rest and change, September 9, 1888.

As we remember how earnestly, untiringly, and in what weakness of body he worked for the Master, these words suggest themselves as particularly appropriate,—

> "Go, labor on; spend and be spent,
>   Thy joy to do the Father's will:
> It is the way the Master went;
>   Should not the servant tread it still?"

DR. A. G. WALLACE.

The family of Dr. Wallace took up their abode in Sewickley in 1884, a valuable addition to the United Presbyterian Church.

Dr. Wallace is statistical clerk of the General Assembly, corresponding secretary of the board of church extension, which aids mission congregations in securing houses of worship, and he is also a member of the editorial staff of the *United Presbyterian*. At the request of Dr. W. L. Wallace, whose health was failing, he supplied the pulpit for six months in 1886; and when, July 1, continued illness caused the pastor to resign, he was "acting pastor" for two years, a pastor in the true sense of the word. To those of his charge who were prevented by illness from attending upon his ministrations in the sanctuary, the words, "sick and ye visited me," came with a new and beautiful significance when associated with Dr. Wallace.

Rev. A. M. Campbell was called to the Sewickley U. P. Church in the autumn of 1889, and remained until the spring of 1892. He is now pastor of a large and flourishing congregation in Princeton, Ind.

The young people's prayer-meeting which is held every Sunday-evening before service, and is so helpful to both old and young, owes its origin to Mr. Campbell's zeal.

When, in the providence of God, the pulpit became vacant during the summer of 1892, the people with one voice gave a call to Rev. Mason W. Pressly, which he, recognizing as the voice of God, accepted. It seemed a fitting tribute to the memory of the venerable founder of the church, that one of his kindred and name should take up the work he began, and with the vigor of his young manhood spend and be spent in the service of Him who called him to the charge.

There are connected with the church several societies for mission and other church work. Besides the two

FIRST UNITED PRESBYTERIAN CHURCH.

ELMER E. MILLER.

Bible classes taught by the pastor and Mr. Robert Trimble, there is a large, flourishing Sabbath-school, of which Mr. Elmer E. Miller is the Superintendent.

Mr. Miller was born and brought up in Sewickley, and is well known both here and in Pittsburg as an architect, and very highly respected in the community as well as in the church, where he fills the positions of elder and superintendent, where he has been a life-long attendant.

The elders have been James Ellis, William Watt, John Thompson, Thomas McGahan, Alexander Miller, William McCoy, Francis McClelland, William Reed, James McGowan, H. J. Murdock, T. E. Wakeham, James W. Arrott, Thomas Hare, John Richardson, Elmer E. Miller, Robert Trimble.

Precious memories cluster around the name of Rev. David R. Kerr, D.D., whose ministrations among the people,—where for many years his lot was cast,—both in the public sanctuary and in the little prayer-meeting, were received with prayerful, loving hearts. Majesty and humility were beautifully blended in his character, and the precious words which fell from his lips are treasured in the hearts of many of the Sewickley people in all the churches.

BAPTIST CHURCH.

In the winter of 1873 the members of different Baptist churches in Pittsburg and Allegheny, in view of the fact that quite a number of families of like faith were residents of Sewickley, called a meeting, to be held in Mozart Hall, to discuss the advisability of making an organization and having regular services. Fifteen names were enrolled as "constituent members."

The firm of "Chamberlin, Thomas, and Boobyer" gave the use of Mozart Hall, free of cost, for Sunday-school and church services, and, after having preaching every Sunday afternoon for three months by city pastors, a council of pastors and laymen was called, an organization effected, and a unanimous call extended to Rev. John E. Craig, of South Pittsburg.

The council, which was held on May 22, agreed to recognize the organization as a "regular Baptist church;" so a charter was applied for, and on June 8, 1873, Pastor Craig began his work.

Mozart Hall was used for four years, during which time there were three pastors; and when, in 1877, Mr. Milford, the officiating pastor, received and accepted a call to New Jersey, this fact, together with the removal of several of the best families in the congregation, was quite a drawback; but for a time service was held every Sunday afternoon, Dr. McKinney, of the Presbyterian Church, residing at Edgeworth, usually officiating. At last, for want of a suitable meeting-place, these services were given up.

The next effort to bring together the members was made in 1888, when it was decided to make a united effort to establish the church—which was still an organized body—permanently. Several Baptist families had removed to Sewickley, so a number of new names were given in, and for a time preaching by supplies was held in Odd-Fellows' Hall.

FIRST BAPTIST CHURCH.

Rev. J. M. Scott was chosen pastor, and it was decided to erect a place of worship. A lot was purchased at the corner of Beaver and Grimes Streets, and as the people contributed liberally towards the fund for the church building, which was soon under way under the supervision of Mr. Charles T. Cooper, who gave his time and labors freely to the work, it was soon completed. It was dedicated in June, 1889.

Mr. Jacob Boobyer, who may be said to be really the founder of the church, says:

" Mr. Scott left us in April, 1891, and for some months we were depending on supplies, to one of whom, Rev. J. W. Moody, we extended a unanimous call, which he accepted, December, 1891, and he has filled the position very acceptably since. Our growth is slow, but the people are united, and we are making progress. Our prayer-meetings are well attended, and we have a good Sunday-school, under the able supervision of Mr. and Mrs. Carey. Our industrial and mission work is another encouraging feature of our church work for the youth of our church and community.

Deacons.—J. Boobyer, H. H. Schenck, J. F. Carey, S. A. Chamberlin, R. B. Boobyer.

Trustees.—J. Boobyer, John D. Britton, L. D. Evans, W. R. Kniss, S. A. Chamberlin.

Secretary.—Charles Kelly.

Treasurer.—Miss Annie Stevenson."

No one has rejoiced more over the success of the new church than Mrs. Sarah Woodburn, whose time and labors for the past few years have been given wholly to church work.

Rev. John W. Moody, pastor of the First Baptist Church, Sewickley, Pa., was born at Middle Rasen, Lincolnshire, England, October 6, 1846. He was educated in an English collegiate institution, preparatory to Oxford and Cambridge. Deprived of the advantages of the higher schools because of feeble health, he entered the profession of journalism early in the teens, and at sixteen was reporter on the *Hull Daily Express*. He was subsequently editor and assistant editor on several English papers, including the *Preston Chronicle*.

When about twenty-three years of age, he came to this country, and after about a year's residence at Trenton, N. J., he commenced the publication of the *Mercer County News*, a weekly paper, which still lives in the city named, and in which he still has a controlling interest. While engaged in this occupation, he commenced the study of theology; the ultimate result being that he was ordained to the ministry in the Baptist denomination, and left the business interest in charge of his brother, Elliott G. Moody, who for many years has edited the paper. He was first called to the pastorate of a small church at Junction, N. J. Two years' labor increased the membership of the church threefold, and during that time another church was organized at Washington, N. J., the result of mission work. From thence he removed to Athens, N. Y., where five years of service produced like good results. From thence he came to Western Pennsylvania, being pastor of the First Baptist Church at Monongahela, Pa. Here he established the *Baptist Exponent*, a denominational paper in the interest of his denomination. This church he left

REV. JOHN W. MOODY.

JACOB BOOBYER, JR.

to devote his whole time to the paper, it having in the meantime been removed to Pittsburg. While supplying the Sewickley Church temporarily, he was called to the pastorate, and commenced his pastoral relation January 1, 1892. Since then he has resigned his editorial position, and now, in conjunction with his duties as pastor of the church, he is engaged in publishing *The Sewickleyan,* a local paper devoted to the social and home interests of the community.

During the pastorate so far about thirty members have been added to the church, and the financial conditions have considerably improved.

COLORED CHURCHES.

There are three congregations of the colored race in Sewickley.

The first is the A. M. E. Zion Church, on Thorn Street. The church and parsonage occupy the ground presented to the congregation by the late Theodore H. Nevin. The pastor, Rev. George W. Lewis, was born a slave in West Virginia, September 25, 1849. When six years old his mother was sold from him, and he has neither seen nor heard of her since. When about ten years of age he was sold to a master in Maryland, with whom he remained until during the War of the Rebellion; in 1863 he left his "so-called master" and went to the Union army. Being rejected as a soldier on account of his youth, he hired himself to Captain Whitney, and remained with him until the close of the war, witnessing many battles. Saying "good-by" to the captain at Baltimore in December, 1865, and being without home or friends, he went to Bedford, Pa., where he worked and educated himself to the best of his ability.

In 1880, Hon. Job Mann sent him to Howard University, Washington, D.C., where he spent five years preparing for the ministry. After graduating in 1886, he took charge of the A. M. E. Zion Church at Mt. Pleasant, and at the end of three years was called to Uniontown, Pa.

He has been in Sewickley two years, and is a highly-respected and successful pastor, an earnest Sunday-school worker, and advocate of the temperance cause. Mr. J. Ward is the Sunday-school superintendent.

George W. Marlatt, who was connected with this church for years, and died March, 1893, deserves special mention. He was born a slave in Berkeley County, W. Va., November 23, 1831. He came to Sewickley in 1864, and was in the employ of Mr. R. H. Davis at Osburn. At his request, Miss Rebecca Davis (now Mrs. Dr. Willard) and her brother, Mr. Swift, taught him to read. Rev. Samuel M. Mackey, of Simpson Chapel, Allegheny, who spent several years on the Davis farm and saw much of this man, says he was one of the most honest, upright, conscientious persons he ever knew. The constant cry of his heart was, "Woe is me if I preach not the Gospel;" and night after night he spent hours in earnest, pleading prayer to the God whom he longed to serve.

Mr. Mackey says "his native eloquence in prayer was something wonderful;" and he feels sure that if this brother had commenced earlier in life as an exhorter, even with the lack of an education, his God-given wisdom would have placed him in the front ranks of the ministry in his own church. He was a happy man when he could read God's word, and at last "satisfied his conscience" by obtaining a license to preach, and as opportunity offered officiated among his people.

Rev. J. M. Morris is the pastor of St. John's A. M. E. Church, on Elizabeth Street, which was dedicated August 3, 1884. He was born in Ohio, educated at the Lutheran College at Springfield, and the Western Theological Seminary in Allegheny. Mr. Morris is a very intelligent and well-educated man, a great thinker, and fluent speaker. The Sunday-school is superintended by Mrs. Jane Johnston.

Mr. Morris has filled many important charges at Oil City, Pa., Wylie Avenue, and East End, Pittsburg, and other places.

Rev. J. W. Kirk, pastor of the "Antioch Free-will Baptist" Church, on Fife Street.

The first pastor was Rev. C. W. Frazier, a missionary of the Western Pennsylvania Association of African Free-will Baptists, who in 1891 organized the church.

Mr. Kirk has been pastor two years. He was born in Northrop, Va., February 14, 1855, and was educated at Storer College, at Harper's Ferry.

We now have eight churches in all, including Methodist, Presbyterian, United Presbyterian, Episcopal, Catholic, and Baptist. The Methodist Church, on Broad Street, the Presbyterian, on Beaver Street, and the Catholic, on Walnut Street, are the only ones that have bells to ring for service. The one in the tower of the Presbyterian Church rings thirty, fifteen, and five minutes before each service. The five-minute bell is always *tolled*, and many persons ask why it is rung in this way. The explanation is this. Soon after Mr. John Fleming's death, the family presented the bell for the new church, as a memorial to Mr. Fleming, and the third bell is always tolled as a tribute to his memory. It bears the following inscription: Presented to the Presbyterian Church of Sewickley, in memory of John Fleming, MDCCCLXX, "*Vivos Voco Mortuos Plango.*"

PHYSICIANS.

Four physicians are associated in our minds with almost everything that concerns the early history of Sewickley,—Dr. John Dickson, Dr. William Woods, Dr. Ellis W. Worthington, and Dr. Alexander Black.

Dr. John Dickson (one of the three brothers so long and widely known as among the leading physicians in the country) was born in Cecil County, Maryland, April 24, 1812. He was of Scotch descent. The history of his family was connected with the records of the State for many generations. His father removed to Clinton in 1821. At the age of sixteen he taught in the public school, at the same time carrying on his studies, walking to Cannonsburg every Friday evening to recite. Dr. Matthew Brown said of him, recognizing his ability, "There goes the most promising young man I know; if he lives, he will make a great name for himself." He began the practice of medicine in 1831, in Sewickley. His office was on Beaver Street, almost on the spot now occupied by the Baptist Church. He was a member of the Presbyterian Church, and of the building committee for the first church. In 1843 he removed to Allegheny.

JOHN DICKSON, M.D.

When travelling through Europe, inspecting hospitals and medical schools, he found the cholera raging in Rome, and devoted his services to the sufferers. During the civil war, he gave himself to his country whenever practicable, and went with the volunteer medical corps to the bloody fields of Chickahominy and Shiloh.

For more than thirty years before his death he resided at Edgeworth, going to the city every day to attend his large practice. His duties in the city did not prevent his being ready at all times, night or day, to visit the sick in Sewickley and the surrounding country, in consultation with other doctors, where his kind, benevolent face seemed always to bring hope and comfort. There were few better botanists than he. To quote the words of another, " He nodded to the four thousand plants within our floral region as to familiar friends, and called them by their names as he would the members of his family."

Dr. William Woods, for many years an elder in the Presbyterian Church, loved and honored, (the mention of whose name recalls some of the most precious and yet saddest memories of our lives,) was a kind neighbor and friend as well as physician. His quiet, composed, gentle manner, as he strove to prepare us for a possible bereavement in store for us, and his own firm faith and trust in a wise, unerring Providence, helped to stay the uprising of rebellious thoughts, as we prayed for strength to say, " Thy will be done." He was born in Allegheny County, in 1804, was the son of a minister of Scotch descent. He located in Pittsburg when he commenced to practise, and distinguished himself for his self-sacrificing devotion to the suffering multitude during the cholera epidemic in

1832. He came to Sewickley about 1843, where he spent almost the remainder of his life.

Dr. Ellis W. Worthington, a licensed Methodist preacher on the circuit including New Brighton and Blackburn, for a number of years studied under Dr. Dickson, and decided to make the practice of medicine his life-work. When Dr. Dickson removed to Allegheny in 1843, Dr. Worthington took his office on Beaver Street. In the midst of his busy life as a physician, he was always ready to fill the pulpit in case of an emergency, and was largely in demand to officiate at weddings and funerals. He went to his reward many years ago, and is less clearly remembered than the others.

Dr. Alexander Black, who for many years was a resident of our borough, was a son of Rev. John Black, of Pittsburg, and a brother of Rev. Andrew and Colonel Samuel Black, all of whom have passed away. His son, Samuel W. Black, resides at Edgeworth. Dr. Black was a thoroughly educated man, having finished his medical studies in Edinburgh, Scotland. Having studied both schools, he practised the allopathic and homœopathic systems, and was a very successful physician.

CHAPTER III.

IN those early days we knew every one by name, and a stranger on our quiet streets was quite an event.

I remember, when I was a child, a neighbor, who often dropped in, and who was, in her way, a wonder for knowing who everybody was, where they came from, and what was their business, came into the house, one day, and said, "I saw a strange woman go down the road; I wonder who she was?" No one could tell her; and the conversation drifted to other things, when again and again she said, "I *do wonder* who that woman was?"

Were she an inhabitant of our thriving town now, she would find herself in just such a quandary very often.

Our village at that time did not boast of a post-office. A mile and a half below the village, a wealthy gentleman, in a room of his fine residence (which, after the lapse of so many years, stands, in its slightly remodelled condition, a comparison with modern dwellings) had a post-office for the accommodation of his friends and the surrounding neighborhood. In this way we received the letters that came in the days before the cheap postal system was introduced, like "angels' visits, few and far between." The few persons who went to the post-office during the day brought the mail for the neighbors.

Mr. Way tells in regard to the early days, of a letter

from Thomas McKean, of Philadelphia, sent August 19, 1809, to John Way, Esq., township of Ohio, Allegheny County, received September 25.

A letter dated Germantown, Pa., February 12, 1812, John Way, Esq., Ohio Township, Allegheny County, 12 miles from Pittsburg. *Postage, 20 cents.*

In 1816, there was a weekly mail between Pittsburg and Beaver, and in 1825 Mr. Shields opened the post-office mentioned above.

At that time a paper was published, called *The American Courier*, in which was published weekly instalments of a story called "Linda Walton; or, the Pilot of the Belle Creole," by Mrs. Caroline Lee Hentz. Like a dream, I remember how anxiously this paper was looked for, and how a little company eagerly gathered around while one of the crowd read aloud the thrilling story. What a proud people we were when we had a post-office of our own, kept in a corner of a grocery store by a teacher of the old Academy. Mr. John Way (now of New Lisbon, Ohio) was appointed postmaster in 1851, and we thought we were highly favored to receive one mail a day; while now it requires a number of persons to distribute the huge budget of mail matter that comes to us eight times a day. When Mr. Way was quite young, in 1840, he walked from his home at Edgeworth to Pittsburg to attend the Harrison Convention, a distance of sixteen miles, by the Beaver Road, winding around the "narrows." Finding there was no boat running next day to bring him home, he walked back.

We owe the first daily newspaper delivery to Mr. Way. In 1846, when he was at the Academy, he and Mr.

JOHN WAY, SR.

David Shields, of Leetsdale, each received a copy of the *Daily Chronicle* by mail, the only daily paper that came to the Valley. In 1855, he engaged a boy, and had the *Evening Chronicle* delivered throughout the village to quite a number of people; many of whom remember this venture very gratefully. There is now a daily sale of the several morning and evening papers of about sixteen hundred copies, besides a very large sale of weekly papers. The news-stand at the station is quite an acquisition to the place; all the leading periodicals and magazines can be procured there.

Theodore W. Nevin, editor of the *Pittsburg Leader*, was born at Edgeworth, July 24, 1854, and has spent all his life in the Valley. He is a son of the late Rev. D. E. Nevin, the first pastor of the Presbyterian Church of this place. He was educated at Sewickley Academy and Western University.

In 1873, he entered the *Leader* office as a printer's apprentice, and in 1875, while still at work in the *Leader* office, commenced to study law. In 1876, he went to Europe to study German and pursue his law studies, but upon his return in 1877 he gave up the study of law, and again entered the *Leader* office as reporter. In 1881–82, he was Washington correspondent of the *Leader;* in 1882, telegraphic editor and associate managing editor. Upon the death of his brother Wilfred in 1887, he was elected President of the Leader Publishing Company.

In November, 1890, Mr. Nevin was married to Miss Bessie Appel, daughter of Rev. Theodore Appel, D.D., of Lancaster, Pa. They reside on Walnut Street.

Mr. Joseph Nevin, brother of Theodore W. Nevin, entered the *Leader* office as travelling agent in 1878, and in 1884 became business manager, which position he holds at the present time, attending to the duties of the position " in a signally efficient and progressive manner." Previous to his connection with the *Leader*, he was in the white lead business. Mr. Nevin married Miss Sarah Cunningham. They reside on Walnut Street near Thorn.

Miss Addie Nevin, sister of Theodore and Joseph Nevin, entered the *Leader* office in 1881, and after several years' experience became Society Editress, which position she still very ably fills. Miss Nevin wrote the "Social Mirror," "a comprehensive and brilliant historical work on the society people of Pittsburg and Allegheny." The book met with marked appreciation by the public. Miss Nevin resides with her mother at the old homestead at Edgeworth.

The house in which the first post-office was kept was the thirty-first house built in Sewickley. It stands near the corner of Beaver and Walnut Streets.

At the end of the house, by the side of a run, stood a large sycamore tree, under whose friendly shade many a happy hour was spent in play by the children of the neighborhood. Returning, after some years of absence, and naturally looking for all the old favored haunts, we looked in vain for the old sycamore tree. Nothing was left but the *stump*. Gazing with sorrowful feelings at the ruin and recalling many scenes of by-gone days, it was a matter of regret that, of all the old playmates, now scattered here and there, not one had been near to say to the ruthless destroyer :

D. L. S. NEELY.

"Woodman, spare that tree,
  Touch not a single bough!
In youth it sheltered me,
  And I'll protect it now."

Our present postmaster, Mr. D. Leet S. Neely, was born at the family homestead at Leetsdale, in 1852. He was educated in the public schools of the Valley and the Sewickley Academy.

His father, Mr. William Neely, is still living at Leetsdale, and has many memories of the "olden time," as he was quite a young man when he took up his abode on the Shields's estate, where he still lives. Mr. Neely was married in 1872 to Miss Harriet Kniss.

What an event the building of a new house used to be. How the neighbors rejoiced at its completion; and it often happened that two or three teams were sent, with many helping hands, to remove the household goods. We never thought of insulting the owners of said teams by offering money for the use of what was freely offered.

A relative of mine had just moved into a new, comfortable dwelling, and the doors were thrown cordially open to friends and neighbors for a regular house-warming. Quite a number of persons from the nearest city came to join in the merry-making. There were games for those who objected to dancing, by which you will infer that we *did* dance. Well, yes; we did! And in the square and French fours and Virginia reels in which our merry feet kept time to the music of the violin, I fancy we were quite as harmlessly employed as those who now take part in the gymnastic exercises so necessary as a source of physical training.

I heard two old friends talking the other day about old times. One of them had been a farmer's daughter, and her father's farm had been a very fine one; and in addition to the apple and peach orchards, and rows of fine cherry trees, there was an abundance of blackberries in the fields. During the conversation, the one who had been a resident of the village said to her friend: " I remember, one day, that Lizzie and I went berrying, and, after we had filled our buckets and were ready to come home, your sister came to call us to dinner. She had killed chicken and baked biscuit while we were picking berries." Her friend replied, " You don't know how glad we always were to see any of you come for cherries or berries; the company far more than repaid us for the trouble of getting dinner."

Some of the finest apple orchards you ever saw were to be found in our neighborhood. What times we boys and girls had gathering apples, and how we enjoyed seeing the rich juice as it was squeezed through an immense press, kept in the orchard of the village inn, and helping to pare the apples and stir the immense kettles of apple-butter which every family annually made. There were no apple-parers in those days, and the work of preparing the apples was no small matter.

During the winter evenings we were allowed, on condition of returning at an early hour, to exchange visits with our young friends, when we cracked nuts, ate apples, and told wonderful stories.

I remember a pretty, black-eyed girl who took part in those narratives. She had one frightful story of a traveller who disappeared in a very mysterious manner in an inn; and one night, just before separating, she said in earnest tones, when asked for her hair-raising story, "I would tell it to you, but I'd be afraid to go home." We besieged her until she did tell it again, and then we raised a little company and took her home.

In these days of quick travel and transportation, you can hardly imagine what our town was like in the days of long ago. Droves of cattle, sheep, and horses passed up our main streets, and, would you believe it, sometimes a drove of turkeys being taken in that way from one city to another. A drove of turkeys *en route* for Pittsburg from the West arrived at Edgeworth, one evening, just at dusk, and, thinking it was time to retire for the night, all betook themselves to the friendly shelter of some trees just across the lane from Edgeworth Seminary. No efforts of the drivers could dislodge them; and they, too, were obliged to seek shelter for the night under the roof of the kind-hearted family owning the grounds, and the next morning proceeded on their way to the city.

Speaking of turkeys reminds me of a true story about a boy who lived on a farm about a mile back of the town. The father and mother of the hopeful youth were regular church-goers; and one morning, just as they were starting for church, a lot of turkeys, of which the housewife was very proud, were making for a field of vegetables, and the father called out to the boy to drive them away, saying, "Tommy, take the *heads* off them turkeys!" then joining his partner, they wended their way to church, hoping Tommy would watch the turkeys.

Imagine their consternation when, on returning, they found he had literally taken off every turkey's head but one. At midnight the good people commenced their Monday's work and prepared the whole flock for market; then, as soon as the work was done, they took a journey of fourteen miles in a wagon to market. This fond mother's ambition was to see her son a minister, but, as he left our town in his boyhood, we cannot say whether he kept on literally obeying his parents or not.

The road out past Tommy's home, which is now a favorite drive in summer, was at that time the route often taken by sleighing-parties. A great wagon-bed was filled with straw and placed on an immense sled, and into it were packed from twelve to twenty boys and girls, and away we went, shouting and laughing, and sometimes singing a merry song, unmindful of oft-repeated orders to keep our mouths shut in the frosty air. In those days of old-fashioned winters, we had a great deal of snow, and plenty of fine coasting down hill on the outskirts of the town; the long pull up hill being far more than repaid by the ride down. I remember that one winter those who had a distance to come to church, who had sleighs or the aforementioned sleds, had the pleasure of using them thirteen Sundays in succession, and during a protracted meeting in the Methodist Church the people came from miles out in the country every night.

The first school in the village was in a small log-house which stood not far from the spring on the Watson property. It had one window, a small opening between the logs, in which oiled paper did duty instead of glass. The teacher was Mr. Scott.

The next teacher, who was the first to occupy the old log church as a school-house, was Mr. Robert McAuley,

who married Miss Mary Mitchell, a sister of Mrs. William Miller, of Lincoln Avenue. Mr. Mitchell was one of the early settlers in Ohio Township, coming here about 1813, and is well remembered by many of the old residents.

The second school-house used in the place was an old log-house, the one mentioned as being used for church service by the different denominations before there was a church in the place. There are very few persons left in the village who remember anything about going to school there.

Among those who received the first rudiments of their education in the old school-house was Milton Browning Goff, son of Philo and Prudence Goff, who were two of the first members of the Methodist Church in Sewickley.

Mrs. Johnston (Mary Goff) now lives in the old homestead, the only member of the family in Sewickley. The old school-house, where her brother Milton first went to school, was just across the street from this old home. Sewickley may well be proud of this one of her sons.

We glean the following facts from the *Western University Courant* :

"Milton Browning Goff was born in Pittsburg, December 17, 1831. Up to twelve years of age he remained in Sewickley, attending the public school and Rev. J. S. Travelli's Academy. He then learned the trade of printer, and worked as compositor on the *Commercial Gazette*. He was noted for his swiftness in type-setting and his knowledge of the art at which he was working. He worked at his trade until 1851, when he entered Allegheny College, at Meadville, from which he graduated in 1855, taking the degree of A. B. In the same year he was elected to the chair of Mathematics and Natural Science at Madison College, Uniontown, and retained his position for two years. On January 1, 1865, he was elected to the chair of Mathematics at the Western University, which position he held for seventeen years, being Chancellor *pro tem.* in 1881. In 1882 he was given the Professorship of Mathematics and Astronomy at Allegheny College, which position he retained until called to the Chancellorship of the Western University in 1884, a position he held until his death.

" Professor Goff was one of the most promising mathematicians in the country. He was the author of seven text-books on arithmetic, the latest of which appeared about a year before his death. He also wrote numerous papers and treatises on astronomy and kindred subjects for the periodicals. In 1858 he received from his Alma Mater the degree of Master of Arts, in 1881 the degree of Doctor of Philosophy, and in 1884 the degree of Doctor of Laws."

Judge White paid him the following tribute : " I knew Professor Goff intimately for almost thirty years. We were members and official members of the Methodist Episcopal Church, Sewickley, most of the time. No man was ever more prompt and faithful in the performance of his duty. I have seen him under trying circumstances, but never saw the first risings of anger or passion. He was always calm, quiet, and self-possessed, with a gentle smile on his countenance. This was not the result of weakness or a cowardly spirit. He was a strong, brave man, with great intellectual strength that kept the pas-

HON. JAMES M. LOUGHRIDGE.

sions in complete subjection. Dr. Goff was never found
on the wrong side of any question. All his instincts and
impulses were in the right direction. He never acted
hastily, or never expressed an opinion without reflection.
Quick in intellect, he always took time to think and
deliberate before expressing an opinion, and when he
made up his mind, the question was finally settled as far
as he was concerned. In all the relations of life,—as
husband and father, as citizen and church-member, as
neighbor and friend,—I never knew one that surpassed
Dr. Goff."

The school-house remembered by many of the men
and women as the place where the foundation for their
education was laid, among whom are Mr. J. McElwain,
Mr. J. J. Ellis, Mr. Samuel Little, Mr. G. F. Muller,
Mr. S. C. Rinehart, and Rev. J. Q. A. Fullerton, is the
old brick building at the corner of Lincoln and Centennial Avenues.

One of the most successful teachers, whose long term
of faithful service left its impress on the minds of many
now scattered far and near, was Mr. James M. Loughridge, whose wife and sister, Miss Maggie Loughridge,
(now Mrs. Aiken, of New Castle,) assisted him.

Some of the best mathematicians of the borough were
pupils in that old school-house; some of Mr. Loughridge's pupils having completed Ray's higher arithmetic
at the age of ten years. He removed with his wife and
two daughters, Rebecca and Carrie, to Oskaloosa, Iowa,
many years ago.

Carrie Loughridge, now Mrs. Bennett, of Oskaloosa,
is the only one left of the family we knew and loved.

Mr. Loughridge died April 20, 1893, aged seventy-two years. After his removal to Iowa, he filled the positions of teacher, county superintendent, mayor of the city, and justice of the peace. His last years were spent in the insurance and real estate business.

Many of them have gone abroad to fill places of honor and trust in the world, and still others, whose lives have seemed one long day of toil and trial, have filled the places of those of whom it is said, "They also serve who only stand and wait."

As the years passed on, younger boys and girls took the places of those who had left, to whom the old school-house became very dear. What wonderful exhibitions these scholars used to get up, when the school-house would be crowded to the door, the youthful performers arrayed in most wonderful costume. Just before my mind's eye there comes the picture of a youth, one of the best managers and most active in getting up these entertainments, as he appeared in a dialogue, crowned with a wonderful wig, as he personated, to the life, the character of a fine-looking old gentleman.

I remember nothing of that dialogue but this character—the *wig*, perhaps, being such a wonder in its way, helps to account for this. School-days have vanished, the youth has grown to manhood, and I wonder if, when he leaves the sanctum where his editorial notes are penned for a fashionable city paper and returns to wife and children in his rural home, he ever tells them of the jolly times "we scholars" used to have in the old school-house.

Another of these youthful performers, a *born* artist,

C. S. RINEHART.

G. F. MULLER.

who had a penchant for "making his mark" at a very early day as an artist,—as school-books as well as doors and window-sills at home could testify,—has, by his apt illustrations in New York and other papers, helped to educate and dispel the blues from the minds of his old school-mates. While his fame has become world-wide, and many persons at home and abroad have been proud to do him honor, nowhere did he and his work receive a warmer welcome than during the reception accorded him in Carnegie Art Gallery, where he exhibited some two hundred of his original beautiful drawings of life and character in many parts of the world he has visited—England, France, Spain, Germany, and his own country ; the reproduction of which in the pages of prominent magazines and art publications has afforded a rich treat to lovers of the beautiful throughout the world. Here also was to be seen his magnificent life-size painting, "Washed ashore," which has been accorded so much praise and honor, both here and abroad, and which places him unquestionably high in the niche of Fame.

A number of concerts to raise a fund for the organ for the new Presbyterian Church (which has done duty about thirty years) were given under the leadership of Mr. R. P. Nevin, by the really fine talent possessed by many of our people, affording a real treat to those who rarely visited the city or attended a public performance of any kind. Among those taking part in those concerts were Mr. John Irwin, Jr., Miss Black, Miss Critchlow, Miss Ritchie, Miss Eliza Shields, Miss Mattie Nevin, Professor John Way, John Way, Jr., Andrew Ellis, James Miller, John I. Travelli, John I. Nevin. A concert was also given by the children under the management of Professor Cornelius, who had singing classes for both old and young.

A song called "The Indian Hunter" was sung by Charles Stanley Rinehart; another, called "Uncle Sam's Farm," by Harry S. Black, and the closing song, a duet, entitled "Good-night and joy surround you," by Tillie McLaughlin and James J. Ellis. Miss Tillie used her fine voice for years as leading soprano in the choir of the Presbyterian Church of this place. She is now Mrs. Kirk, of Cannonsburg, Pa.

Laura Rinehart, a little dark-eyed, curly-haired girl, who was a leading singer among the little ones, is now the wife of a far-famed organist; and her own rich, cultivated voice has again and again delighted large cultured audiences. The quiet, composed, perfectly self-possessed manner with which she sang to the large crowd of friends and relatives the song,—

> "What fairy-like music
> Steals over the sea,"

which, after all these years, I seem to hear her sweet voice still carrolling through the little old church, was prophetic of the ease and power with which she has oftentimes since sung to crowded houses in the different halls and churches of Pittsburg and vicinity. During the summer, while with the family enjoying the lake breezes at a summer resort, she sings for the pleasure of friends at the hotel, and many times by request in the church. Realizing that her wonderful voice is a God-given talent, she uses it in His service.

WILLIAM S. DICKSON.

Mrs. Gazzam's private school on Thorn Street is remembered with pleasure by many persons.

I think one of the old pupils voiced the sentiment of all who remember that as their first school when she said, lately, "Everybody loved Mrs. Gazzam." I remember as some of her pupils, Hannah Nevin, Lidie Nevin, Mary and Susie Hopkins, Mary Woods, Laura Rinehart, Annie Jones, Milly Shields, Birdie Dickson, Eliza Travelli, and Mary Travelli. While her school-work endeared her to the hearts of her pupils, she is remembered by many others as engaged in *every* good work.

THE PUBLIC LIBRARY.

The public library owes its origin to the enterprise of Mr. William Dickson, who, realizing the need of such an institution, agitated the question, until in 1873 a reading-room and library were opened, which supplied a long-felt want of the people.

Aside from the membership fee of five dollars yearly, public entertainments netted a sum that added materially to its support.

After being removed from one room to another, it was removed in 1880 to the public school-house, where the books were distributed free of charge to any inhabitant of the borough.

The reading-room has been discontinued, but it is hoped that when the new school-house, now in course of erection, is completed, this feature will be renewed.

The first officers were:

President.—John Way, Jr.

Vice-President.—William Dickson.

Secretary.—E. R. Kramer.

Treasurer.—John Thomas.

Mr. Wm. Dickson was born in Glasgow, Scotland, and came to Sewickley in his childhood, where he has since lived. He was married in 1871 to Miss Agnes M. Miller, daughter of Mr. William Miller. She died about a year ago. Mr. Dickson has been a successful contractor.

Our old school-houses have been replaced by new ones; our old churches have given way to new and costly structures; our once dark and muddy streets are paved and brilliant with electric lights; many improvements have been made for the pleasure and comfort of the people, and yet there are those in our midst who think "the former times were better than these," and long and sigh, alas! in vain, for their return. The following words find an echo in the hearts of such:

" Afar o'er the hill-top the day, robed in splendor,
　　Comes forth like a queen from the realms of the sun:
And the valleys uplift the white veil of their slumber
　　To welcome the dawn of a day just begun.
The dew-spangled lawn and the glittering forest
　　Drop gems at my feet and o'er-jewel my head;
But I long for the freshness and joy of the mornings
　　That came with the beautiful days that are dead.

" The sweet vanished days that went out with the sunset
　　Shall find me alone in the land of my dreams
With the friends and the songs and the flushes of gladness,
　　And your skies mirrored fair on the silvery streams.
Shall the heart never mourn for a song that is silent,
　　When the sweetest of harmonies o'er it are shed;
Shall the dark buried past find no bright resurrection,
　　Shall eternity bring back the days that are dead?"

HOMER JAY ROSE, A.M.

The substantial school-house that had served for so many years on Thorn Street was destroyed by fire, February, 1893, and a new building, which will be one of the finest in the country, is in course of erection on the beautiful lot where the other school-house stood. The lot is bounded on three sides by three of the principal streets,—Broad, Thorn, and Chestnut,— and will be quite an ornament to the town.

The Principal, Professor Homer Jay Rose, A.M., was born in Pine Township, Mercer County, Pa., October 29, 1856. He received his first education in the district schools, was a student of Pine Grove Academy, and a graduate of Edinborough State Normal School.

After teaching several terms in the country districts and five years in Grove City College, he became Principal of the public school at Parker's Landing, serving three years; was two years Principal of the Emlenton schools, and the last four years has been at the head of our Sewickley schools.

Professor Rose is noted for sterling honesty and uprightness of character, and is a faithful, earnest, and, above all, Christian worker. He was married in 1880 to Miss Margaret J. Shaw. Their residence is on Centennial Avenue.

CHAPTER IV.

HEN Sewickley was laid out, Division Street, (then called Graveyard Lane,) which divided the two farms which included all that is known as Sewickley Borough, was one of the principal streets. It extended from the grounds now known as Fleming's grove to the grounds owned by Mr. Osburn, on Bank Street.

At the lowest termination of this street, a plot of ground was given to be a free graveyard for the town. There was very little rambling about on Sunday in those early times, but we often on Sunday summer afternoons went to that old graveyard, sometimes reading our Sunday-school books under the shade of the old trees, and never failing to read all the inscriptions on the old tombstones, on which were many Scripture verses. It was a beautiful spot, with its lovely evergreen trees, and there is associated with its memories nothing of dread or fear; but the place seems even now to be hallowed ground. The other burial-spot was just back of the old Presbyterian Church, not used in such early times as the other, and yet many precious ones were laid to rest there. In 1860, a site was chosen for a cemetery, to which after

240

HON. D. N. WHITE.

a time the silent inhabitants of the two graveyards were removed. November 1, 1860, was the day appointed for the dedication of the cemetery. It was a lovely, bright day, although so late in the season. A platform had been erected and seats prepared for the large company that had assembled. The exercises were commenced by a short prayer by Rev. J. S. Travelli. A hymn was sung, and an address delivered by Rev. Henry Baker, of the Methodist Church. After this address, a hymn was sung, composed, music and words, by our talented townsman, Mr. R. P. Nevin, whose music and speeches had helped to inspire the leaders in many a political campaign. Ah! how many of the young men whose voices united with his in the memorable Fremont song are now silently sleeping in that city of the dead, and yet they are forever young, tuning their voices in nobler strains. A dedicatory prayer, by Rev. James Allison, and the benediction, by Rev. John White, closed the exercises.

DEDICATORY HYMN.

BY ROBERT P. NEVIN, ESQ.

As pilgrims on the barren waste
  Of dreary desert, sands astray,
With anxious heed and earnest quest
  Anticipate the doubtful way,
And, timely, with the night in view,
  Seek ere the day leans to its close—
Thoughtful of ease through toils yet due—
  Choice stead for shelter and repose;

Here, followers through a wilderness
Of paths uncertain and remote,
While we a kindred aim confess,
A kindred care, Lord, we devote ;
To meet the need that lies beyond,
And harbor seek to shield us best,
When life's last task of service owned,
We gather to our final rest.

Thanks to Thy name, Almighty One!
For the sure promise Thou dost deign,
That the deep slumbers thus begun,
Shall, waiting cease, not wait in vain ;
That darkness, silence, and the pause
Of still oblivion shall have end,
And fair above the night's stern awes
The dawn of a new morn ascend.

Sleep—only sleep : no ruder doom ;
No vital wrest with wrest of breath ;
No bane, suppressless, to consume,
Nor death—as doubters dream of death !
Sleep—only sleep ; shut for a space
From the world's troublous sphere of strife,
To wake, regenerate, heirs through grace,
Of resurrection and of life !

Thus with the rapturous faith at heart
That challenges distrust and fear,
Stayed by the pledge Thy words impart,
Lord, we approach Thy presence here !
Own Thou our mission, hear our plea,
That this our chosen camp of rest,
Protected by Thy watch may be,
And by Thy generous favor blest !

ROBERT P. NEVIN,

Forever be these shelters sure,
  Warded from peril and from harm.
These sylvan solitudes secure
  From rude obtrusion and alarm ;
Forever hallowed, nor profaned,
  And, by our rite devoutly paid,
Be thou the warrant ! hence ordained
  Forever sacred to the dead !

Mr. Nevin is a brother of the late Rev. D. E. and T. H. Nevin. He was educated in Chillicothe, Ohio, Sewickley Academy, and Jefferson College, where he graduated in 1842. For a number of years he was engaged in the drug business, at the same time writing articles for *Knickerbocker, Atlantic, Lippincott's,* and other magazines. He was also, for years, editor of the *Leader,* then of the *Times* in Pittsburg.

Hon. D. N. White, while he was identified with all the public interests of the place, deserves especial mention in connection with this cemetery. He was the very founder of it, its superintendent, and did more than any one else to make it the beautiful place it is. With a will that surmounted all obstacles, he toiled on in this work, sure of the success that at last crowned his efforts. His death removed one of Sewickley's best men.

As time sped on, new houses sprang up in many places, many more families came to settle here, and new faces were seen on our streets. What a feeling of prosperity and security there was. How proudly fathers and mothers looked upon the children in their homes, and with what a fond hope for the future did they think of the sons and daughters grown to maturity.

When the civil war broke out, it seemed hardly possible that any of "our boys" would be called to go; but, as the cloud grew blacker and the conflict waged fiercer, a company was organized and the boys began drilling. The new Presbyterian Church, which was just roofed and floored, was used for this purpose, and night after night, parents and sisters, sweethearts and friends, gathered in as spectators.

The Sunday before the company left to be mustered into service, they attended morning service in the Presbyterian Church and evening service in the Methodist. In the evening, as they walked two by two up the aisle to their allotted pews, the congregation sang,

"There is rest for the weary."

On the forenoon of the day they left, July 6, 1861, they assembled, in company with many friends, in the Presbyterian Church, when beautiful swords were presented to Captain Meyers and Lieutenants Shields and Nevin. The presentation speech was made by J. W. F. White, Esq. Each man in the company was at the same time presented with a New Testament, and addressed in appropriate terms by Rev. James Allison. They took the afternoon train for the city, to go from thence to Philadelphia. That day was one never to be forgotten. With breaking hearts, amid forced smiles and many tears, the relatives and friends bade them good-by.

> "Brave boys were they.
>   Gone at their country's call;
>   And yet, and yet we *could not* forget
>   That many brave boys must fall."

They left Pittsburg the same afternoon for Philadelphia, and were mustered into service July 11.

MUSTER-ROLL OF SEWICKLEY COMPANY.

Captain, Conrad C. Meyer.
First Lieutenant, William C. Shields.
Second Lieutenant, John J. Nevin.
Orderly Sergeant, W. R. Stokes.
First Sergeant, George Grady.
Second Sergeant, James O'Rourke.
Third Sergeant, Robert M. Irwin.
Fourth Sergeant, Nicholas Way.
First Corporal, John D. Tracy.
Second Corporal, James Cooper.
Third Corporal, T. J. Hamilton.
Fourth Corporal, James D. Travelli.
Fifth Corporal, Wm. Cameron.
Sixth Corporal, Albert Moore.
Seventh Corporal, Luther N. Guy.
Eighth Corporal, Samuel B. McKown.
Fifer, Abraham McCray.
Drummer, Alexander Ingram.
Wagoner, Philip Emmert.
Wagoner, John Trunick.

Joseph Ball.
E. Bendenburg.
W. K. Boyle.
Benjamin Bryan.
John T. Boyle.
Peter Conway.
George Carson.
Wm. Callahan.
Henry Chessman.
Barney Connolly.
Stephen Conwell.

John B. Crownover.
J. B. Cochran.
John S. Dickson.
John Donahoe.
James Dalzell.
H. H. Doyle.
Wm. Dugdale.
George Davis.
Albert Earle.
Nelson Edwards.
Bernard Friel.

James Grady.
W. R. Gibson.
James Grimes.
Benjamin Grimes.
A. J. Gray.
Wesley Hamilton.
J. R. Hendrickson.
J. L. Hendrickson.
Lawrence Hackett.
Alexander Hill.
James Hard.
W. H. Hutson.
P. S. C. Hough.
Oliver Johnson.
Robert Johnson.
Wm. Johnson.
Leonard Kolp.
R. H. Kelly.
Wm. Lucas.
Thomas A. Linn.
Patrick Malone.
John Marlatt.
John Moore.
Joseph Moore.
P. W. Miller.
John McDonough.
John McElheny.
A. McFadden.

Wm. McGahen.
Patrick McGilley.
Wm. McKindley.
Wm. McClintock.
James Nugent.
Daniel Norris.
Adam Ocks.
John O'Connor.
Albert Person.
John Park.
James Richey.
Charles Richey.
Henry Rhodes.
F. G. Sherbourn.
Thomas Smith.
Patrick Smith.
Moses Sherman.
Jacob Sherman.
Charles Thrasher.
Wm. Taylor.
George Thornburg.
John Trunick.
Joseph Vogler.
W. H. Wilson.
Jacob Walbert.
Wm. Wharton.
Archie Wharton.
Wm. Wardrop.

John Welsh.

In a letter dated August 8, 1861, one of the boys said, writing from Camp Geary, Sandy Hook, Md.:

"We have now been under canvas four weeks, and, if I may judge from that small term of experience, I think the evils of camp-life have been greatly exaggerated by anxious friends at home;" and again, "The progress of our regiment from Camp Coleman to the southern confines of Pennsylvania was a constant ovation. When we entered the cars at Philadelphia for Baltimore, the people thronged us with profuse offerings of bread, butter, cheese, coffee, etc.; bareheaded women came up, pressing upon our acceptance their eager gifts, until, with all, our stuffed and crammed haversacks could contain no more. Strangers shook our hands like old friends, and with tears in their eyes invoked God's benediction upon us and our mission. This scene was repeated, on a smaller scale, at every station. You can imagine the influence of such a valedictory upon impressionable young men gathered, like those of our company, from country villages. The remembrance of such farewell scenes serves to hedge around the soldier's heart with a strong sense of the sacredness of his cause, and really, I believe, to shield him, in some measure, against evils otherwise considered inseparable from camp-life. The scenery around our encampment here is grand and beautiful. Lofty mountains fling their shadows down upon us, and send us grateful breezes, while at our feet flows the narrow Potomac,—at our feet, figuratively speaking, for it is really inaccessible to us, as our pickets forbid all approaches to its cool, inviting waters."

Thoughts of the absent soldiers were mingled with the duties of every hour; anxious thoughts as to their comfort and privileges. Their vacant places in the different churches to which they belonged suggested the thought that they were deprived of all religious privileges, but some of the words written by one of our

soldiers in a Southern camp seemed to answer and set
at naught this anxiety :

> 'Tis not alone within
> The gorgeous fane, rich with the blazonry
> Of man's device, that God is to be found ;
> He heard the humble suppliants cry alike
> From land and flood, from burning desert waste,
> And from amid the icy battlements
> That glitter 'neath the Arctic skies.   He hears
> His children's cry from leafy mount and from
> The quiet vale, where every Sabbath morn
> The voice of prayer and melody is heard
> Amid the whispering trees, that seem the while
> To listen by the rippling stream unto
> Each thrilling strain.
>
> God's church is in the camp!
> Blest thought, that half obliterated the pang
> Of separation from the dear ones far away ;
> That lightens all the soldier's toils ;
> That soothes his sorrows, and that makes him look
> Unfearing, in a holy cause, upon
> The race of danger and of death! Blest thought!
> Triumphantly it floats on angel wings
> Above the bristling bayonet's flash, the roll
> Of battle-must'ring drum, the booming roar
> Of cannon, and the clash of arms within
> The battle's dead affray !
>
> Shut out from all
> The world, afar from home, with no kind voice
> To charm the lonely hour, no loving hand
> To soothe him on his couch of pain, no ear
> To listen to his last faint words in death,
> Where shall the soldier look for hope, for peace, and
>   comfort there?

Thank God! religion is
Not bound; 'tis free as air of heaven! Where'er
Life's pulses throb through feeling, human hearts,
Its sweet and holy power is felt. It comes
Unto the camp, where iron-hearted men
Have gathered at their country's call to fight
For Justice, Home, and Liberty! and hearts,
Which never felt its influence before,
Are brought in a mysterious way to feel
And own its blessed sway.

Henceforth the camp,
Divested of its former character
For vice and immorality, shall be
Redeemed unto the cause of virtue ;
While men shall stronger, purer, better grow
Within its school of patience, manly toil
And danger."

Long letters from home, and many tokens of remembrance, many articles of food to vary their plain
fare, and articles of clothing, were sent by those at
home.

A band of girls, under the leadership of Miss Rebecca
Way, met in the Presbyterian Church week after week to
sew flannel shirts for the boys, and many a heart-sick,
longing sigh and anxious thought were given to those
who were risking their lives under "the starry banner,"
while they strove to cheer each other in their work. How
we miss the bright smile and kind words of this, one of
the noblest and best of women, who gave herself so untiringly to work for the soldiers, since the Master called her
"up higher;" but the fragrance of her holy life still
lingers.

Mrs. Gazzam was another one whose prayers and

time and strength were given to the soldiers. In company with a young friend, she walked to "Fair Oaks" from Sewickley every month, collecting by the way the sum, great or small, that each person was willing to give to help buy food and clothing for our own and other soldiers. Many other noble women gave themselves to this "labor of love."

The first death in Company G, Sewickley Rifles, was that of A. Jackson Gray, just six months from the day he left Sewickley. A daily paper contained the following notice:

"DIED.—At Camp Goodman, Point of Rocks, Md., January 6, 1862, Private A. Jackson Gray, Co. G, 28th Regiment Pennsylvania Volunteers.

"At a meeting of the company, the following resolutions were adopted:

"*Resolved*, That we, his fellow-soldiers, tender our sincere sympathies to his family in their bereavement; for, as they have lost an affectionate son and brother, so have we lost a kind and cheerful comrade, and our country a good man and true.

"*Resolved*, That although he was denied the death that a soldier covets—that of the battle-field—and suffered that which alone he shrinks from—a death by disease, far from home,—yet he did his duty, fought long and well against the hardships of the wintry picket, and gave up his young life for his country as gloriously and well as those who have the privilege of dying for it on the field of glory; for 'They also serve who only stand and wait.'"

The news of this death seemed to touch the hearts of the people and lead them to work more and pray more for those who were left, during the months of suffering and anxiety that followed.

The second death in Company G was that of Joseph Moore, brother of Mr. Alfred A. Moore of the same company. He was attacked with typhoid fever, and after a short illness died in the "General Hospital" at Frederick City, Md., March 14, 1862. He was buried in the National Cemetery at Frederick City.

Although his brother did not arrive until two days after his death, he was comforted by knowing that all that loving hands could do to smooth the pillow of the dear one had been done, and he returned to the post of duty cheered by the hope of a joyful reunion in "the land of peace and joy," when all the trials and battles of this earthly life are over.

How eagerly the daily paper was looked for, and with what fear and dread, after the news of a battle, were the lists of "Killed, wounded, and missing" eagerly scanned. Sometimes it was laid aside with a prayer of thanksgiving that the dear one had been spared, and again it was cast aside with a bitter wail of anguish, and a cry for strength to the God of battles for grace to say, "Thy will be done," as the records revealed the fact that heart and home were made desolate. What a crushing blow was that which fell upon us when the news came that at the battle of Antietam, fourteen months after the company had left home, in addition to many wounded, three of the boys had been killed.

Of all the dark days of that cruel war, of the many trying scenes through which the people passed, none left so deep a shadow as the one on which the bodies of James D. Travelli, John Dickson Tracy, and William C. Richey were brought home and buried in our new cemetery,—three boys who left home that bright day in July, hoping soon to return. Services were held in the Presbyterian Church, which was crowded to overflowing.

The services were introduced by singing a part of the one hundreth Psalm, after which a portion of Scripture was read by the Rev. A. Williams, D.D. Prayer was offered by the Rev. David McKinney, D.D., followed by an address by Rev. L. R. McAboy, D.D., and another by Rev. James Allison, pastor of the Presbyterian Church. Rev. Robert Hopkins then offered a prayer, which was followed by the singing of the hymn commencing,

"O Thou, who driest the mourner's tears,"

and Dr. Williams pronounced the benediction.

The vast assemblage then mournfully proceeded to the cemetery. A detachment of the "Leet Guards," under Captain R. P. Nevin, acted as a guard of honor to the bodies of the departed soldiers. An address was made and a prayer offered at the grave of James D. Travelli by Dr. McAboy. Mr. Allison made the address and offered prayer at Charlie Richey's grave, and Rev. Robert Hopkins read the burial service of the Methodist Church at the grave of John D. Tracy. Three volleys were fired by the military, and the great assemblage returned to their homes, every heart touched with grief and sympathy.

The same month, William I. Nevin, who had a short time before left college and enlisted, thinking his country needed him in her sore extremity, died in the hospital at Washington, and his body was brought home and buried in the Sewickley cemetery.

A Washington correspondent writes to a Pittsburg paper:

"The oldest son of Theodore H. Nevin, of Sewickley, died here to-day. I judge he was about twenty-one years of age. He was a member of the famous artillery company known as Hampton's Battery, to which belonged also a son of Professor Williams, a son of Dr. Finley, two sons of Mr. Marshall, of the foundry, Pittsburg; young Heberton, a son of Mr. Noble, the upholsterer, and several others like the above, of the finest young men of your city. Young Mr. Nevin came here with the battery from Front Royal some four weeks ago. They camped in an unwholesome spot, and several of them were soon attacked with typhoid. Mr. Nevin alone has died, the others being now decidedly on the mending hand. His father and Dr. Finley were with him in his last moments. This is a great affliction. May God make this severe providence work for good to the sorely-smitten hearts that now bleed under the blow."

As one after another fell from the ranks, others rose up to take their places. Some who were such mere boys when the first call was made, that no one thought of their going, now enrolled their names beside their brothers; while others, whose families were dependent wholly upon their work, hesitating before, now, in the hour of their country's growing necessity, tore themselves from home and fireside and joined the ranks.

Among these were: Harry Sterling Black, Alexander Watson Black, James J. Ellis, William Beverland, William I. Nevin, Ellis Scott, Albert White, William A. Ellis, Henry Nash, William Douglass, Joseph Douglass, John

Neely, James Buckley, J. J. Scott, Milo P. Scott, A. W.
P. Richey, Sample W. Brooks, Thomas Boyd, Thornton
Goff, David McKinney, M.D., Fielding Goff, Wm. For-
rester, Madison Bonham, Thomas Stevenson, John Park,
John Holsinger, Edward Holsinger, Robert M. Ingram,
Samuel Grady.

One boy of fifteen, upon hearing that an older brother
had died of wounds received in battle, found a place as
fifer for the company, the youngest but one soldier in
the State. Every means possible was resorted to in order
to raise money for soldiers' supplies. Fairs were held in
many places, and the Sanitary Fair, in Allegheny, was
the means of raising a large amount of money. Gov-
ernor Curtin was present at the opening of the fair. The
following items appeared in a daily paper, in an article
speaking of the opening night :

"Numbers 9 and 10 are the booths in which are displayed 'Sewickley's offering,' and a highly creditable one it is, too. It will
be remembered that the children and ladies of the Sewickley
Valley lately gave a local fair, which realized the handsome sum
of four hundred and eighty dollars for the Sanitary and Subsist-
ence committees; but the ladies have been working like beavers
since, and, besides contributing very largely in money, refectory
material, etc., they have gotten up a very beautiful display of all
sorts of useful and fancy articles. Among other things, we noticed
a very rich and stylish dressing gown and smoking-cap, some ex-
quisitely embroidered children's dresses, collars, and articles of
ladies' wear; a splendid and costly afghan; some magnificent
photographs from Mr. Dabb's gallery, and innumerable other
articles both useful and ornamental.

"The Misses Kramer, Way, Shields, Wardrop, Nevin, Knox,
Jones, Finley, Davis, Taylor, Adair, Thompson, Miller, Cass, and
Dickson, together with a number of married ladies, attended at

this table by turns, and are doing everything possible to exhibit the merits of their wares.

"They have fixed the prices of all the articles exceedingly low, but little above the cost of material, and expect, therefore, to sell them off at an early day, and without resort either to raffling or auction.

"The Sewickley department is one of the most attractive in the 'Bazaar,' and all visitors should give the articles a close inspection. They will stand it well."

When at last the dreadful war was over, and all the need of toil and sacrifice at an end, those who were left of all that had joined the different regiments were about to return home, the glad words, "The *boys* are coming home!" were often hushed by the thought that many who had left their homes would never return.

"Soon shall the voice of singing
    Drown war's tremendous din;
Soon shall the joy-bells ringing
    Bring peace and freedom in.
The jubilee bonfires burning
    Shall soon light up the dome,
And soon, to soothe our yearning,
    Our boys are coming home!

"The vacant fireside places
    Have waited for them long,
The love-light lacks their faces,
    The chorus waits their song:
A shadowy fear has haunted
    The long deserted room;
But now our prayers are granted—
    Our boys are coming home!

" O mother, calmly waiting
   For that beloved son!
 O sister, proudly dating
   The victories he has won!
 O maiden, softly humming
   The love-song while you roam—
Joy, joy, the boys are coming,
   Our boys are coming home!

" And yet, oh, keenest sorrow!
   They're coming, but not all:
Full many a dark to-morrow
   Shall wear its sable pall
For thousands who are sleeping
   Beneath the empurpled loam;
Woe! woe! for those we're weeping,
   Who never will come home!

" O sad heart, hush thy grieving;
   Wait but a little while!
With hoping and believing,
   Thy woe and fear beguile;
Wait for the joyous meeting
   Beyond the starry dome,
For there our boys are waiting
   To bid us welcome home."

One of the number of the Sewickley boys who left home that July afternoon, after many experiences and changes, was at last taken prisoner. After months of terrible suffering in "Libby," he returned to home and friends, and the church in which that little company, of which he was lieutenant, had drilled in preparation for active service, was crowded to the door to hear his experiences of prison life. I remember he began his lecture by saying, "In the first place, I was not asleep," as it had been reported that, being overcome with fatigue and want of rest, he had fallen asleep by the way-side, and thus been captured. Certainly no one slept during that lecture, and those who for so many years read his editorials in the Pittsburg paper which he so ably conducted, knew him as a very wide-awake man, with more than an ordinary amount of intellect.

A beautiful monument in our cemetery commemorates the deeds of valor and self-denial of our dead soldiers. Upon the front face of the monument an inscription within a laurel wreath reads:

> " ERECTED,
> BY THE
> CITIZENS OF SEWICKLEY,
> IN MEMORY OF THEIR
> VOLUNTEER SOLDIERS
> WHO SACRIFICED THEIR LIVES
> FOR THE
> UNITY OF THE REPUBLIC
> IN THE WAR OF THE
> GREAT REBELLION,
> 1861 TO 1865."

On the south face, within the typical laurel, we find:

> " KILLED IN BATTLE.
> Lieutenant Wm. C. Shields,

Wm. Banks,	John D. Tracy,
Wm. Painter,	James D. Travelli,
Robert White,	Wm. C. Richey,
Theodore Webb,	Robert Johnston,
Wm. Wharton,	Thomas Smith,

> Moses Sherman."

On the third side we come to this inscription:

"DIED OF WOUNDS AND DISEASES.
Captain Alexander McKinney.

James Scott,	James L. Grady,
John Park,	Albert J. White,
Joseph Moore.	Andrew J. Gray,

Henry M. Rhodes."

And on the fourth side:

"DIED OF WOUNDS AND DISEASES.
Wm. I. Nevin,

Thomas A. Hill,	W. H. Forrester,
Harry Black,	G. W. Forrester,
Alex. Black,	James Grimes,

L. B. Gainer."

The winged embodiment of Fame presides over all on the marble shaft. She holds the trump of fame in one hand and the laurel wreath in the other.

The Fourth of July after the close of the war was inaugurated by a salute at daybreak of three guns, four guns at sunrise, and a national salute at eight o'clock.

The Sunday-school children, after assembling at the different churches, formed into a procession, under command of Captain David Shields, and marched to the grove of Mr. Cochrane Fleming. The citizens and visitors then assembled in the grove, and the following programme was carried out:

PRAYER.

REV. WHITE.

SINGING BY CHURCH CHOIRS,—"*America.*"

READING OF THE DECLARATION OF INDEPENDENCE,

W. A. COLLINS,

of the *Chronicle.*

COLONEL JOHN I. NEVIN.

SINGING,—" *The Prisoner's Hope.*"

ADDRESS TO THE CHILDREN,

REV. MR. LOCKE.

SINGING,—" *The Prisoner's Release.*"

ADDRESS OF THE DAY,

REV. DR. BITTINGER.

SINGING,—" *Victory at last.*"

ADDRESS IN MEMORY OF OUR SOLDIERS,

J. W. F. WHITE, ESQ.

SINGING,—" *Sleeping for the Flag.*"

Refreshments were served to the children at noon, and a dinner of substantial refreshments to the grown people.

After a few hours of recreation, the crowd reassembled at the grand stand, to hear the reading of the Emancipation Proclamation, and an address by Rev. Joseph S. Travelli. Some of the toasts and sentiments given and responded to were the following:

"The War of 1812: honor to the few surviving soldiers of that struggle."

Response by Squire Sample, of Lawrence County, who related some of his experiences in that struggle.

"A chip of the old block: James T. Sample, who lost a leg in the Mexican war."

Mr. Sample responded by singing, "Nicodemus was a part of the salt of the earth." The audience joined in the chorus. Music.

" The man that hath no music in his soul,
Is fit for treasons, stratagems, and spoils."

Responded to by Mr. R. P. Nevin.

A number of patriotic addresses were made. At nine o'clock a fine display of fire-works was exhibited from the lot above the railroad station (just opposite the telegraph office), accompanied with the firing of artillery.

Gradually the ranks of the returned soldiers have been thinned out as disease claimed its victims, but faithfully, year after year, those who are still left to wage the battle of life, in company with many Grand Army men from the city and many of our citizens, march to the cemetery to strains of music, and

> "Gentle birds above are sweetly singing
>   O'er the graves of heroes brave and true,
>   While sweetest flowers we are bringing
>   Wreathed in garlands of red, white, and blue."

Many a tear falls in loving remembrance as some of our leading men speak eloquently of the days and the scenes that saddened many homes in our Valley. Appropriate music is rendered by the choir, lead by Mrs. J. Sharpe McDonald, who has had the honor of being made a member of the Grand Army.

A band of the wives and sisters of "the boys" prepare a sumptuous repast, which is spread in our town-hall, at the close of the day; and after the inner man is regaled by the delicacies prepared, a "camp-fire" is held, and young and old listen to the reminiscences of bygone days. At such times, we look in vain for those who were the leaders in all such work years ago, but their work on earth is done.

This chapter, so full of war and those associated with

the soldiers, would not be complete without speaking
more fully of Mrs. McDonald, who, besides being for so
many years closely identified with all the musical interests
of the borough, has so freely given her time and labor to
make the memorial day arrangements a success, as well
as to everything connected with the Grand Army, in
which her wonderful musical talent could be used. For
twenty-one years, as the thirtieth of May rolls around, in
sunshine and storm, she has never failed to be present, to
mingle her tears with those who pay their loving tributes
to the memory of the departed heroes, both here and
in the cemetery where lie the loved ones from the city
homes, and in sweet, soul-thrilling music to lift the
thoughts of the mourners beyond the scenes of time and
sense to the land of peace and joy. While Sewickley
has reason to be very grateful for the many and great
kindnesses received at her hands, through the use of the
God-given talent used for His glory, alike in scenes of
joy and sorrow, nothing has endeared her so much to
many hearts as her work in connection with the Grand
Army.

The following quotation from an address delivered at
a memorial meeting of Hays Post, G. A. R., on August
29, 1881, explains her being a member of the Grand
Army, and is a fitting close to these pages about our
"soldier boys" and the brave women who have been
associated with them:

"To-night, my comrades, there is with us one who,
for the past eight years, has been unremitting in her
attention to the interests of Post 3, of the Grand Army.
No Decoration day has passed without her sweet voice

being joined in the sad ceremonies of that day. At a meeting of the Post, a series of resolutions was adopted.

"In accordance with the resolution, this beautiful badge of the Grand Army has been made, and to you we present it as a slight token of our respect and esteem; and whilst intrinsically it may not be valuable, yet the thought that you are the first and, I may say, the only female who has ever received this emblem, should in itself prove to you how highly you are held in the estimation of the comrades of Post 3.

"Take it, and with it the love, respect, esteem, good wishes, and prayers, not only of comrades of this Post, but of every member of the Grand Army that knows of your goodness and kindness to us."

CHAPTER V.

SWEET peace dwells in our midst. To the younger portion of our community, the war with all its sad history seems shadowy and unreal. They can hardly realize, either, the changes that the past years have brought. For the benefit of such let us review a few of the incidents connected with some of our greatest improvements.

In the winter of 1848–9, Mr. Solomon W. Roberts succeeded, through the efforts of Mr. John Hutchinson, a member of the legislature, (brother of the late Frank M. Hutchinson, of this place,) in getting a charter for the proposed Pennsylvania and Ohio Railroad. Mr. Roberts then went to Ohio, and succeeded in getting his bill through the legislature there; returning, making speeches at all the towns along the proposed route, as to the benefits to be derived from the fulfilment of the new undertaking.

Mr. D. Newton Courtney, whose influence secured much of the right of way for the new road, (a wealthy resident of the East End, Pittsburg,) along with Mr. Roberts, had the supervision of the road during its construction. On July 4, Mr. Courtney, as conductor, took out the first train. Shortly afterwards, he was made "master of transportation," a

position which he held for a number of years. The
high esteem in which he was held by the employés
of the road, was shown by their presenting him with
a valuable gold watch and chain. On the watch was
an excellent engraving of the well-known Courtney
homestead, still standing at Emsworth. Mr. Courtney's connection with the road, afterwards called the
" Pittsburg, Fort Wayne, and Chicago Railroad," lasted
over a period of more than eighteen years. He is
an uncle of Mrs. James McKown and Mrs. Edward
O'Neil, whose families are well known in Sewickley.

You can hardly imagine the excitement attending the
making of the railroad, or the effect the sight of the first
train of cars had upon those who had never seen such a
thing. Almost every one in the village went down to the
railroad about the time the train was expected to pass,
all anxious to see the strange sight, as very few persons
here then had ever seen a railroad. Well! the train
came along, and just at the foot of Broad Street, where
our beautiful new station now stands, the engine gave a
shrill, wild scream that sent almost every one flying back
to the fence or up Broad Street.

Among the crowd was a lady who had travelled on
many railroads ere taking up her abode in Sewickley,
and when she looked around, after the train had whistled
to stop, not a person was near her but the little boy she
had held in her arms, who, after giving a frantic spring,
clung to her for dear life.

It had been promised that the cars would be running
on July 4, 1851. The passenger train was not ready,
but, true to their word, General Robinson, President of

SEWICKLEY STATION.

the road, and some of the stockholders, had some gravel-cars seated by laying boards across, and took a trip to Economy, *the end of the line*, where a sumptuous repast was prepared for them by the Economites.

When the passenger trains commenced running, we had two trains a day, also one freight train. Think of this, you who grumble if a train is ten minutes late, when we now have sixty-four trains in all, arriving and departing from the station every twenty-four hours during the week, and seventeen on Sunday. The car-fare then between Allegheny and Sewickley was twenty-five cents for a single trip, and a quarterly ticket ten dollars.

Upon arriving from Allegheny, after a day spent in shopping and seeing the sights, it was a very common thing to hear persons say to each other, on alighting from the train; "Why, were *you* on the cars?" scarcely realizing that a fellow-passenger could travel near and not be known, as they always were on boat or stage.

For a long time after the railroad was in operation, some of the residents still preferred travelling by the river route. The trip to the city was always a holiday, and the sail on the river much pleasanter, they thought, than the *very short* ride on the cars.

One day, an old lady, who had come from somewhere back in the country to take the train for the city, meeting a friend struck up a conversation. The train was about to move off just as the conversation was becoming interesting, and our friend called to the conductor, waving her hand excitedly, to "wait a little." Some of the by-standers, taking in the situation, hurried her off.

Mr. Samuel McCleery, of our borough, who was at

18

that time a merchant of New Brighton, being burgess of the borough, used his influence that the right of way might be secured, and with the co-operation of Edward Hoops, Silas Merrick, Squire Chamberlin, Dr. Stanton, Benjamin Rush Bradford, and others, was successful. Appreciating Mr. McCleery's efforts on behalf of the new road, a committee waited upon him three times, composed of the leading business men of the Beaver Valley and Pittsburg; General Robinson and the directors; and the engineers, among whom were the late Frank M. Hutchinson and William P. Shinn, J. D. Layng, and Edward Warner, and urged him to accept the position. He was about starting for Chicago, with a view to opening up a mercantile business with Pittsburg, but decided to accept the position thus urged upon him, and commenced duty, March 25, 1852. Mr. Lake, who was an engineer on the Pennsylvania Road, was placed in charge of the train, which by this time ran from Pittsburg to New Brighton. Mr. Andrew Morrow and Mr. Wm. Beeabout were brakesmen and Mr. Andrew Hoag, baggage-master. Mr. Morrow afterwards became baggage-master, and for the past thirty-two years has filled the position of conductor. He is well-known to our citizens who travel on the trains as the soul of honor and faithfulness to duty.

Mr. Beeabout's sons are now connected with the road in different positions, while Mr. Hoag is a wealthy merchant of Steubenville.

A few days after the train, with its newly-appointed force, had begun to run, the first trouble with the road was experienced. There had not been such high water since

SAMUEL McCLEERY.

the flood of 1832 as that April rise; the ground at Leetsdale and many places below was entirely submerged. When the train, which had been ploughing its way through the deep water, stopped at Beaver Station, the question was agitated as to the advisability of going on; but it was decided not to make the attempt. While still discussing the matter, the newly-made road, at a distance of about two hundred feet from the train, plunged into the mouth of the Big Beaver, completely filling the outlet lock of the Beaver Canal, so that the road was submerged behind them to the depth of several feet. The train with its occupants was "quarantined" for two days, at the end of which time, the water having subsided somewhat, the train returned to Pittsburg.

The first *collision* on the road occurred about fifty feet from Osburn Station, near the residence of the late General Cass. The cause was this: an eastward bound freight train had stopped at Haysville to take on water, when a westward bound train, loaded with iron for the completion of the road, came along. After a time it was decided to back the freight train to Sewickley, as the dense fog that morning made it dangerous to try to go on. The passenger train due at the time had reached Sewickley, and J. W. F. White, Esq., T. H. Nevin, D. N. White, and others, had come aboard, when, as if by *inspiration*, (as he said afterwards,) Conductor McCleery advised his engineer to run very slowly, no faster than a walk, through the fog. He had reached the baggage-car, had his hand on the inside of the door, when suddenly the backing train struck *their train* and he was sent flying the length of the car. Happily no one was much hurt, had merely a good shaking up.

Upon the opening of the road to Fort Wayne, it was thought best to have an agent in the East to work up and advertise the new road, and Mr. McCleery was chosen. He was very efficient in this work, but after a year's faithful service he returned.

After he had decided to give up his railroad work, he became associated with Wm. H. Smith, formerly editor of the *Post*, and Joseph R. Hunter, one of Pittsburg's best salesmen in the grocery business. Continued ill-health caused him to seek a home in the sunny South, and he purchased a sugar plantation about eighty-five miles from New Orleans, on the Bayou Teche, near the farm of the celebrated Joseph Jefferson, the actor; but at the end of three years he returned with his wife and four children to Sewickley.

In spite of the reverses which came from the loss of the oil refinery, in which he was largely interested, on Herr's Island, during the great "oil flood," his perseverance carried him through, and now he is one of Sewickley's wealthy men. Mr. McCleery married Miss Sheet, of Salem, who comes of a highly intellectual family, counting three ministers and five lawyers among its members.

The first station-house was a shed, made of rough boards. It stood just across the track from where the telegraph office is now, and the hapless passengers often rubbed their benumbed fingers as they waited for a train "overdue." The next station was quite an improvement on this. It was built on the opposite side of the track, a

JOSEPH W. WARREN.

small frame building, on the spot where a *third* station, a brick building now used as a freight depot, stands.

We had a ticket agent in the second station, Mr. Samuel Garrison, who also sold confectionery for the accommodation of the patrons of the road.

Mr. Joseph W. Warren, the present station-master, has filled the position since 1859. Nothing further is necessary to tell of his faithfulness to duty, and the perfect satisfaction with which he has filled the position, than the number of years he has served. Mr. Warren climbed the telegraph pole, cut the wire, and set up the instruments for the telegraph service in the frame station that took the place of the one first mentioned. How the people did crowd around the window when they heard the click, click, and saw the movement of Mr. Warren's fingers, wanting to know all about his *sewing-machine.* The first pay message that was received was from Cleveland, sent by Mr. Cochrane Fleming to the family at home, one day in August, 1859, to have the carriage to meet him on the arrival of the evening train.

The success of the public library was the result of Mr. Warren's energy. When president of the board of school directors, knowing the fund for the support of the library was getting very low, he offered to get up a dramatic entertainment to help tide them over their difficulty. He showed such marked ability in this line, that year after year the people greeted his entertainments with such enthusiasm that through his efforts $1000 have been added to the fund, making the village library an insured success.

All the officials at the Sewickley station are kind,

polite, and obliging, always ready to give information to the public, and to attend to every duty.

The accommodations for travel are better here than even the suburban towns of Chicago, making it as convenient for business men to live here as anywhere on the outskirts of Pittsburg. Ministers, judges, doctors, lawyers, and editors are here in great numbers. Our main street, it is often remarked, reminds one of a fashionable watering-place, from the number of carriages, phaetons, carts, and drags that pass up and down on summer evenings.

Sewickley was incorporated July 6, 1853. Those who have filled the office of Burgess since Sewickley became a borough are the following persons,—Robert Hopkins, David R. Miller, Alexander McElwain, S. D. Miller, T. H. Nevin, William Harbaugh, R. McCready, John Thompson, D. N. White, Robert Watson, F. M. Hutchinson, James Woodburn, G. W. Cochran, Samuel McKelvey, William Stanton, J. Kidd Fleming, William Miller, Albert Moore, Van R. Smith, R. J. Feltwell, J. B. Reno.

Our present Burgess, Hon. George H. Anderson, is now serving his third term. He was born in Pittsburg, in 1832. He was trained to the tanning and leather business, and although a successful business man, his talents and his ability to fill important public positions being appreciated, he was chosen for one position of trust after another. His career as State senator, to which position he was elected in 1870, and filled for six years, is well and favorably known, being made speaker of that body in 1873. From 1877 to 1881 he was postmaster of Pittsburg. He is Vice-President of

HON. GEORGE H. ANDERSON.

the Pittsburg Chamber of Commerce. For the past twelve years he has been actively engaged in the firebrick business. Mr. Anderson was married in 1854 to Miss Nancy H. Darsie, only daughter of Hon. George Darsie. They reside on Grant Street.

SEWICKLEY WATER SUPPLY.

Among the early recollections of Sewickley are many connected with the old wells and springs which furnished a bountiful supply of water for the inhabitants.

How people open their eyes in wonder sometimes, when we tell them of the long walks that had to be taken to the well or spring, as the case might be; and many stories are laughingly told of the chance (?) meetings at the side of one old well, famed for the icy coldness of the sparkling fluid poured from "The old oaken bucket that hung in the well," where *Isaac* met the fair *Rebecca* that henceforth was to gladden his heart and home. As the village increased in size and population, the water supply proved inadequate for the wants of the scattered population, and cisterns for holding filtered rain-water were introduced. The first one made in the village (in 1853) was for Mr. James Ellis, soon after the completion of his new house on Beaver Street, at the head of Chestnut. The clear, cold, soft water was prized very highly, and was eagerly sought in cases of sickness. Dr. Alexander Black, a near neighbor, used it in the preparation of his medicines, and during the last illness of Dr. Worthington, the nurse would allow the use of none but the *healthful rain-water.*

During a long-continued dry spell, when the cisterns, of which there were soon quite a number, were almost empty, how the people eagerly watched the gathering clouds and longed for the showers that often passed over the hill towards Pittsburg or some other favored spot. When the lightning's flash and roar of thunder, followed by the patter of "rain on the roof," assured us we were not to suffer, these sounds were as music to our ears.

A still increasing population and the dread of fire, for which no provision was made, caused the people to agitate the question of having water-works, and supplying the town with water from the springs scattered so plentifully over the hills; so, in 1870–71, the project was carried out. One hundred acres of ground were purchased, and under the supervision of engineers Ediburn and Cooper the work was completed, at a cost of $95,000.

John Patton, Jr., was elected superintendent, which position he ably filled until 1892, when Mr. Henry Nash was elected. The supply is sufficient during the winter months, but there are quite a number of families who use cisterns, some filled with filtered rain-water, others with a supply of the delicious spring water procured in March, which is cool and clear all summer. An arrangement is being made at quite an outlay to procure filtered river-water for the use of the large population, with its increased demand during the summer months.

We had no public hall in early days, and our performances that were not thought to be suitable for the church, were given either in the school-house or in a large room used generally by a wagon-maker for keeping wood. Well! this room had been cleared out, cleaned, and seated

JOHN PATTON, JR.

with chairs and benches, one evening, ready for a performance to be given by a Mr. B., a sort of mesmerist. Almost every one in the village was present. An old lady, who was very conscientious about the places of amusement she attended, said she was a little bit worried and ashamed at finding herself among the expectant audience, until she noticed her minister and his wife there. Mr. B. gave every one who would accept a piece of money with a hole in the centre, upon which they were to gaze as a preparation for the mesmeric state. His manœuvres did not have much effect for a time; at last a young man was pronounced to be in the desired state. We all knew Sam to be the jolliest boy in school, and ready for all sorts of fun and frolic both in-doors and out; and it did seem strange that he should be so *impressionable*.

With an air of triumph, Mr. B. called upon every one to notice this young man, how completely under his control he was; and forthwith began to lead him around and put him through numerous queer performances. Most obediently Sammy followed, his will apparently entirely merged in that of his guide. Slyly opening his eyes a little way and seeing the leader's back turned, he threw up his hands and made such fearful grimaces that quite an audible titter was heard over the room. When Mr. B. turned around, Sam's face was sober as a judge's, and he obediently went through some more wonderful tricks. At every possible chance, when, through the half-opened eyes, he knew he was safe, he repeated his antics; but, alas! Mr. B. turned and caught him once. The crest-fallen man soon brought the performance to a close after this.

Once in a long time the place was enlivened by the coming of a show, usually a menagerie and circus combined. The wagons containing the actors, the animals, and everything needed in connection with the great performance usually came from Pittsburg by way of the Beaver Road, and the tents were pitched in "Grimes's field," at the corner of Beaver and Fife Streets.

Once some real Indians came and gave a performance, which was so different from the usual shows that came here that everybody was delighted. Before the performance began, a number of the men rode on horseback, *single file,* up Beaver Street, and just as the leader was in front of Woods's drug store (or the spot where it now stands) he turned, facing the others, and gave a fearful yell, which we understood was the "warwhoop," and then they all went flying like the wind towards Osburn, and were soon out of sight.

How we did like for a long time after that to go to the woods and practise that yell, where there was no one to reprove us for making a noise, and only echo to answer.

We have an opera house now, and home as well as foreign talent contributes to the entertainment of the people in their thirst for pleasure by concerts, theatricals, etc., some of the people who once frowned down a dance, and thought it a sin to wear a bow of ribbon on their bonnets, being seen within its walls in holiday attire.

An occasional game of ball was indulged in by our boys in earlier times, but now ball games are of frequent occurrence, and there are games of tennis in our athletic grounds almost every day during the summer. These grounds were formally opened in 1882.

ATHLETIC GROUNDS.

As the season rolls round for the annual county fair, the grounds are crowded by a gay, interested party of friends and relatives, who, after patronizing the different booths, the country store, and post-office, witness from the grand stand the races, rejoicing with the victors and valiant knights.

In this connection we must speak of the

SEWICKLEY VALLEY CLUB.

A meeting was held on Tuesday evening, February 16, 1886, at the residence of Mr. William Stanton, Sewickley, for the purpose of organizing an association for the advancement of social amusement in Sewickley Valley. Mr. William Stanton was chosen chairman, *pro tem.*, and, on motion of Mr. A. B. Starr, the following committee on permanent organization was appointed by the Chair, viz.: Mr. A. B. Starr, Mr. Gilbert A. Hays, Miss Theta Quay, Miss Jessie Long, Mr. Frank C. Osburn.

The committee submitted the following report on permanent organization:

President.—Mr. Wm. Stanton.

Vice-President.—Mr. A. B. Starr.

Recording Secretary.—Mr. F. E. Richardson.

Corresponding Secretary.—Mr. G. F. Muller.

Treasurer.—Mr. James Adair.

At the third meeting, held at the residence of Colonel David Campbell, the election of committees resulted as follows:

Executive Committee.—Messrs. A. B. Starr, Frank Semple, O. S. Richardson, D. S. Wolcott, Geo. H. Woods, F. L. Clarke.

Membership Committee.—Mrs. John Tate, Miss Martha Fleming, Miss Clara Campbell, Mrs. Wm. Stanton, Miss Annie McKelvey, Mr. H. M. Richardson, Mr. T. H. B. McKnight.

Amusement Committee.—Mrs. A. B. Starr, Mrs. G. A. Gormley, Mrs. D. S. Wolcott, Mrs. W. A. Baldwin, Miss Theta Quay, Miss C. Whiting, Miss Mina Shields, Miss Juliet Warden, Miss Eva Muller, Messrs. Robt. Wilson, G. A. Hays, G. F. Muller, R. J. Cunningham, James Adair, J. J. Brooks.

The society decided soon after its organization to begin the entertainments with a dramatic representation, which was given at Choral Hall, May 18, 1886. This was followed during the summer by a lawn fête and a picnic. Choral Hall, which after the first few meetings was fitted up for the use of the club, has been used year after year.

Many of the old members have been married or removed from Sewickley, while some have been called to leave the scenes of earth.

The present officers are:

President.—Frank Semple.

Vice-President.—O. S. Richardson.

Treasurer.—J. C. Chaplin.

Recording Secretary.—E. P. Coffin.

Corresponding Secretary.—J. M. Tate, Jr.

Committee.—Mrs. Burrows, Mrs. Rose, Miss Anderson.

THE ODD-FELLOWS.

Sewickley Valley Lodge, No. 692, I. O. O. F., was duly instituted January 4, 1870, under a charter granted by the Right Worshipful Grand Lodge of Pennsylvania, and under date of November 16, 1869, said charter having been granted upon the request of the following applicants:—John McDonald, A. J. Murray, John H. Marlatt, Wm. Ague, James M. Douglas, Paul F. Rohrbacher, Robert N. Brockunier, Eli L. Mushrush, Frank Eberle, John M. Cooper.

At the meeting held (January 4, 1870), the following Grand Lodge officers dedicated the hall and instituted the Lodge (which then met in C. G. Woods's Hall, corner of Beaver and Broad Streets, now occupied by Sewickley Council, No. 170, Jr. O. U. A. M.).

The first election of officers was held January 4, 1870, and the following were elected:

N. G.—John M. Cooper.

V. G.—James M. Douglas.

Secretary.—Eli L. Mushrush.

Assistant Secretary.—A. J. Murray.

Treasurer.—P. F. Rohrbacher.

During the twenty-three years of its existence, the Lodge has had a membership ranging from forty-two to fifty-nine members, and at present has a membership roll of fifty-two.

Shortly after the institution of the Lodge, it was decided to change the name; consequently, by a resolution, same was changed to J. Sharpe McDonald Lodge, No. 692; but owing to a decision of the Grand Lodge a short time thereafter, that the retention of a name of any living being for a Lodge was absolutely forbidden, the name was again changed to its original, and so remains.

From the original place of meeting the members

deemed it advisable to make a change; so arrangements were made, and the hall of Chamberlin, Thomas, and Co. secured (now occupied by the Knights of Pythias and other societies) about 1873 or 1874. In 1879 they removed to the hall of J. McElwain and Co., corner of Beaver and Division Streets, where they have since remained.

Friday of each week meetings are held, from April 1 to October 1, at 8 P.M., from October 1 to April 1, 7.30 P.M. Visitors always welcome.

The following are the officers for the term from April 1 to October 1, 1893:

N. G.—William D. Shearer.

V. G.—Edward D. Sawyer.

Secretary.—W. E. Patton.

Assistant Secretary.—S. Y. McFarland.

Treasurer.—William Beverland.

" We admit within our walls only those who possess good moral character, and who believe in the existence of a Supreme Being, the Creator and Preserver of the Universe.

"Sectarianism and politics are topics excluded by our laws from our meetings, and we have resolved only to know and to love each other as men and brothers.

"To do the work of an Odd-Fellow, we must attend the couch of the sick and dying, the side of suffering and distress, the house of mourning, the grave of the departed, the abode of poverty and want, and visit the widow and the fatherless in their affliction; and also the lodge-room, where social intercourse and fellowship ever abound."

KNIGHTS OF PYTHIAS.

Sewickley Lodge, No. 426, was instituted May 5, 1874, with the following officers:

P. C.—F. A. Meyers.

C. C.—Geo. M. Gray.

V. C.—James Robinson.

P.—J. H. D. Gray.

K. of R. and S.—John S. Grady.

M. of E.—Joseph Ague.

M. of F.—David Duff.

M. at A.—Geo. W. Rhoads.

Trustees.—F. A. Myers, Edward Merriman, John S. Grady.

Representative to Grand Lodge.—F. A. Meyers.

The present officers are:

P. C.—William Leight.

C. C.—William R. Hunter.

V. C.—D. C. Crease.

P.—C. T. Cooper.

K. of R. and S.—R. W. McPherson.

M. of E.—D. W. Challis.

M. of F.—James Shearer, Jr.

M. at A.—Geo. W. Cook.

I. G.—Walter Lockhart.

O. G.—Philip Doughty.

Trustees.—W. J. Grady, S. Y. McFarland, J. F. Nash.

Representative to Grand Lodge.—John B. Lake.

Meets every Tuesday night at Pithian Hall, corner of Beaver and Broad Streets.

KNIGHTS OF HONOR.

Sewickley Lodge, No. 1105, Knights of Honor, instituted May 24, 1878, meets the second and fourth Monday nights of each month.

The Knights of Honor is a fraternal beneficial society. It insures its members in sums of $2000, $1000, or $500, as they may elect, at a minimum cost. The society has been in existence for more than twenty years, and is in a growing, prosperous condition, having paid the widows and orphans of its deceased members $43,000,000 in that time. The following are the officers:

D.—R. B. Boobyer.

A. D.—C. F. Nevin.

V. D.—E. R. Kramer.

R.—Dr. M. S. Burns.

F. R.—B. C. Christy.

T.—S. A. Chamberlin.

Medical Examiner.—Dr. R. McCready.

JUNIOR ORDER UNITED AMERICAN MECHANICS.

In 1887 an application was made for a charter in order to start a Council of the Junior Order United American Mechanics, the following names appearing on said application:

Charles T. Cooper, Dr. Wm. M. Johnston, H. L. Carroll, W. J. Miller, H. L. Warren, Frank Grimes, S. A. Patton, S. T. Shoop, S. Y. McFarland, B. F. Campney, Jr., A. C. Walker, W. H. Schlumpf, E. B. Gray, E. W. Campney, Raymond H. Tea, Dr. F. H. Smith, W. C. Duncan, and Dr. J. B. Chantler.

Owing to considerable delay in procuring a charter, the State Council officers issued a dispensation for the institution of the Council; accordingly, it was instituted June 2, 1887. On July 21 following, the charter was duly received.

The Council was instituted in Chamberlin & Boobyer's hall, corner of Beaver and Broad Streets. Originally the meetings were held on Thursday evenings, each week, but by a resolution and permission from State Council, the time of meeting was changed to Monday evening.

From April 1 to October 1, meetings are held at 8 P.M., and from October 1 to April 1, at 7.30 P.M.

In 1889 the Council moved to the I. O. O. F. hall, but the year following removed to their present council room, corner of Beaver Street and Lincoln Avenue.

The following were the officers for the term beginning April 1 and ending October 1, 1893:

Councillor.—Wm. M. Dryman.

Vice-Councillor.—Jay McCaughey.

Recording Secretary.—Wm. H. Schlumpf.

Financial Secretary.—W. E. Patton.

Visitors always welcome.

General Alexander Hays Council, No. 275, Jr. O. U. A. M., was instituted November 21, 1888, with a membership of sixty.

The popularity of the Council was so great, and the object of the order so noble and patriotic, that the membership increased rapidly, until it numbered two hundred and thirteen. The meetings of this Council, as a rule, are well attended, and the interest and enthusiasm displayed speak volumes for the patriotism of the members.

The Council was named for the illustrious and brave General Alexander Hays, the father of our fellow-townsmen, Alden T. and Gilbert A. Hays.

The Council is officered at present as follows:

Junior Past Councillor.—W. L. Day.

Councillor.—Clark McPherson.

Vice-Councillor.—J. B. McPherson.

Recording Secretary.—J. B. Chantler.

Assistant Recording Secretary.—J. D. McQueen.

Financial Secretary.—G. F. Barkwell.

Treasurer.—George W. Beatty.

Warden.—Walter Lockhart.

Conductor.—James Shearer.

Inside Sentinel.—Park Bonham.

Outside Sentinel.—W. J. Stewart.

Trustees.—W. L. Day, James Shearer, J. D. McQueen.

Committee to Advisory Council.—T. H. B. Patterson, J. D. McQueen.

Sewickley Conclave, No. 93, Improved Order of Heptasophs. This is the second and successful effort to run a Conclave in Sewickley. The first one surrendered its charter, owing to a non-attendance of its officers and a lack of interest of its members.

This Conclave took the old Conclave's number (93), and has so far been very successful, there being a slow growth owing mainly to the fact that there are so many secret societies in our borough.

Our Conclave was organized December 5, 1889, by two very energetic and prominent members of the society,—Mr. H. R. Larimer and Mr. Martin Schroeder, of Pittsburg.

R. J. MURRAY, M.D.

JOHN D. McCORD, JR.

Our first officers were:

Past Archon.—L. L. McClelland.

Archon.—F. H. Smith.

Provost.—D. Leet S. Neely.

Prelate.—W. M. Drynan.

Financier.—O. L. Schlumpf.

Secretary.—Charles D. Richardson.

Treasurer.—Robert Ruttkamp.

Inspector.—Frank Scott.

Warden.—H. L. Hegner.

Sentinel.—George H. Rudisil.

Medical Examiner.—J. B. Chantler.

Trustees.—George S. Cotton, W. M. Gibb, F. L. Stevenson.

Present officers (1893):

Past Archon.—R. J. Feltwell.

Archon.—Daniel Challis.

Provost.—Philip S. Doughty.

Prelate.—Fielding B. Goff.

Financier.—O. L. Schlumpf.

Secretary.—Charles D. Richardson.

Treasurer.—George H. Hegner.

Warden.—D. R. Scott.

Sentinel.—Bernard Simon.

Medical Examiners.—J. B. Chantler, S. D. Jennings.

Meet second and fourth Thursdays of each month, at Conclave Hall, corner of Beaver and Lincoln Avenues, Sewickley, Pa.

I am indebted to the secretaries of the Valley Club and the secret societies for the foregoing information.

The past forty-two years have given us the railroad,

telegraph and telephone, a post-office, a library, paved streets, gas and electric lights, the water-works, natural gas, and last, but not least, a *bank.*

Those who formerly hid their treasures in out-of-the-way places, of which they sometimes laughingly told, or carried them to the city for safe keeping, can now deposit them where he, who for twenty-five years has been the faithful sexton of the Presbyterian Church, has been chosen to keep watch that " thieves do not break through nor steal."

Dr. R. J. Murray was chosen president of the bank by those who had long known and trusted him. He was born in Pittsburg, in 1845. He is a son of the late Captain John Murray, who, after he retired from business as a river-man, lived on the farm a few miles back of the borough, where Dr. Murray spent his boyhood.

Captain Murray was of Scotch-Irish descent. He and his wife (formerly Miss Eliza Graham) were active members of Blackburn Methodist Episcopal Church.

Dr. Murray attended school in Sewickley and Pittsburg, then read medicine with Dr. McCready, of this place, and Dr. Maury, of Philadelphia. After graduating from Jefferson College, Philadelphia, he located in Sewickley, where he has an extensive practice. His wife, who died in 1886, was a daughter of the late Rev. Robert Hopkins, of Sewickley.

John D. McCord was chosen as general clerk in the bank. He is a son of the late William M. McCord, of Pittsburg.

Not directors alone, but school-mates and friends rejoiced at the selection of one so thoroughly trusted and

JOHN B. VAN CLEVE.

respected. We trust many of these will live to see, in the changes that the coming years shall bring, our young clerk filling the position of president of *one* of the Sewickley banks.

When Mr. McCord left the position in the Sewickley bank, April, 1893, to fill the position of teller for the Pittsburg Trust Company, Mr. John B. Van Cleve was elected to the position, which he very ably fills.

Mr. Van Cleve was born at Beaver Meadow, Carbon County, Pa., and is a brother of Rev. R. S. Van Cleve, for many years pastor of Leetsdale Presbyterian Church. He was married to a daughter of Rev. Daniel Miller.

Mr. Van Cleve enlisted as Orderly Sergeant in the 24th Pennsylvania Volunteers, 6th Army Corps, Army of the Potomac. In 1862 he was promoted to Second Lieutenant, and in 1863 to First Lieutenant. He was engaged in the battles of Yorktown, Williamsburg, Fair Oaks, Malvern Hill, Chantilly, Antietam, Fredericksburg, Chancellorsville, Gettysburg, Wilderness, Cold Harbor, Petersburg, and Cherry Run, and honorably discharged August 26, 1864.

After sixteen years' connection with the Pennsylvania Railroad, Mr. Van Cleve taught in Mr. Way's Academy, and gave private instruction, previous to his accepting the position in the bank.

Since the advent of natural gas, there is nothing to obscure the vision of loveliness that meets the eye as we view from a hill to the north-east the town lying at our feet, and the smaller towns on the other side of the Ohio River.

The absence of public works gives an air of quiet

and repose that is very grateful to the tired workers as they return after a day of toil in what we once called the smoky city.

One hundred years ago the red men had possession of this lovely Valley, the first white settler had not yet built his rude cabin.

Could Henry Ulery return to his old haunts, he would scarcely be persuaded that the farm he once tilled was now dotted with stately mansions with beautifully kept lawns. The tread of many feet on the streets where once the echo of his footsteps sent the timid deer fleeing to a place of safety, the shrill scream of the steam-engines on river and railroad, would be a source of alarm and wonder. The encroachments of the river at each flood have gradually carried away the spot on which his primitive home was built on the brink of the river. Only one familiar object would greet his eyes, and yet that is changed,—the *old well*, which, although "a commotion in the earth," as an old resident says, caused every other well to cave in, did not shake the solidly built walls; but the windlass and "the old oaken bucket" are gone, and a modern pump brings up the cool, clear, sparkling water to refresh the weary traveller, as of yore.

Could one of the present inhabitants return one hundred years hence, what changes would he find!

May each one who reads these memories of our beloved Valley so live that his influence shall be felt for good, and

> "So hear the solemn hymn that Death
> Has lifted up for all, that he shall go
> To his long resting-place without a fear."

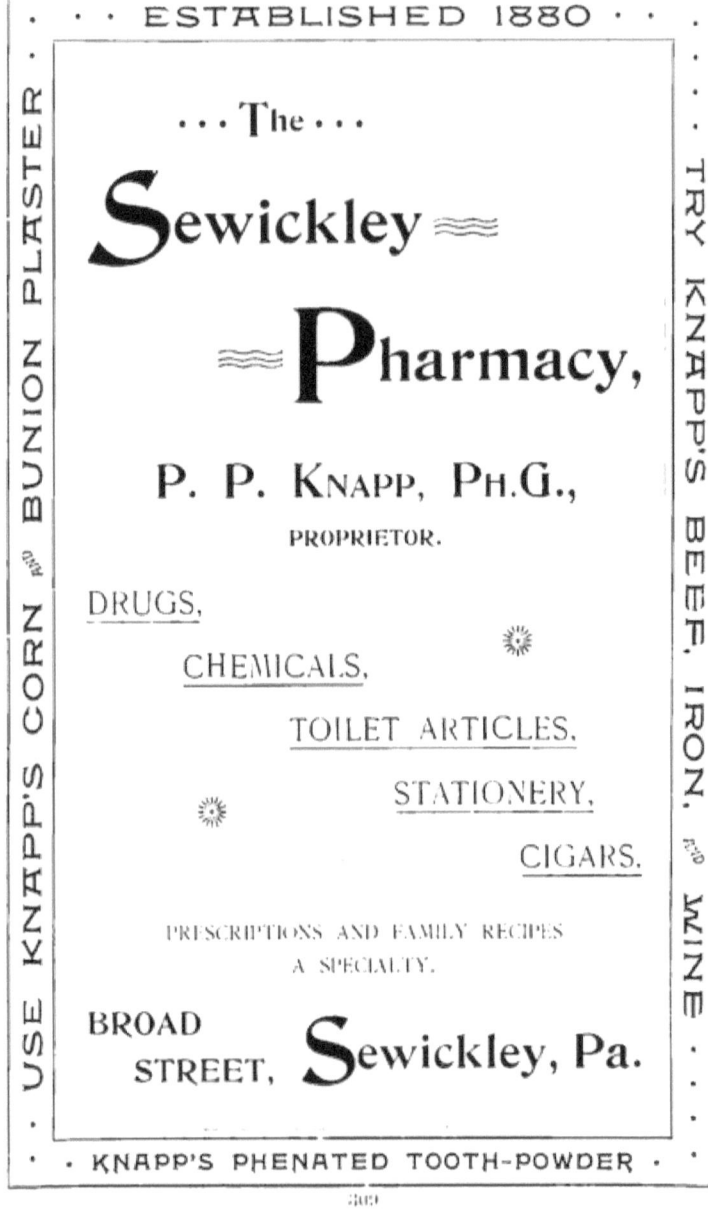

THE
MANHATTAN LIFE INSURANCE COMPANY

Is one of the stanchest and most highly esteemed of the fiduciary institutions not only of New York city, but of the whole country, and it will soon occupy its new gigantic edifice, which is to be one of the most notable structures on this continent.

Its height from the sidewalk on Broadway to the foot of the flagstaff will be about 350 feet. The ground space covered will be 67 ft. x 125 ft., and the building will be a feat in construction heretofore unknown. It is to be supported on piers sunk to the solid rock, 55 ft. below Broadway, the method of sinking being by means of caissons operated by the pneumatic process. The building will contain about 160 offices, exclusive of the Company's quarters, which will occupy the sixth and seventh floors. The Broadway front will be Indiana limestone, and the structure throughout will be absolutely fire-proof. The style of architecture adopted is the Italian Renaissance, enriched in keeping with the best examples of that style.

JAMES C. McKOWN, Manager,
PITTSBURG, PA.

312

314

JOHN B. LAKE,

BUTCHER AND DEALER IN

Beef, Veal, Mutton, Pork, Sausage, Bologna.

HOME DRESSED MEATS EXCLUSIVELY, AND
ALL KINDS OF DRESSED POULTRY.

Beaver Street,   SEWICKLEY, PA.

WILLIAM DICKSON,

Contractor

RESIDENCE:

Thorn Street West of Walnut,

BOX 173.   SEWICKLEY, PA.

ALDEN F. HAYS,

DEALER IN

ANTHRACITE AND BITUMINOUS COAL AND COKE,

Lime, Common and White Sand, Plaster of Paris, Hair, Lath,
Cement, Salt, Sewer Pipe, Fire Brick, Fire Clay,
Grate Tile, and all varieties of

TERRA-COTTA WARE.

Baled Hay and Straw.   Heavy Hauling and Ploughing promptly done.   Artificial Ice.
Orders sent by Mail will receive immediate attention.

Telephone No. 30.   SEWICKLEY, PA.

D. W. CHALLIS,

❄ Contractor ❄

CONCRETE AND SURFACE PAVEMENTS, GRADING,
DIGGING OF CISTERNS, CELLARS, ETC.

HEAVY HAULING A SPECIALTY.

Address P. O. Box 217.   SEWICKLEY, PA.

www.ingramcontent.com/pod-product-compliance
Lightning Source LLC
Chambersburg PA
CBHW060536030726
47498CB00004B/1216